MW00586178

A NOVEL BASED ON THE LIFE OF

PIETRO BELLUSCHI

THE JUDICIOUS USE OF INTANGIBLES

W.A.W. Parker

The Judicious Use of Intangibles: A Novel Based on the Life of Pietro Belluschi is a work of fiction. Some incidents, dialogue, and characters are products of the author's imagination and are not to be construed as real. Where real-life historical figures appear, the situations, incidents, and dialogue concerning those persons are based on or inspired by actual events. In all other respects, any resemblance to actual persons, living or dead, events, or locales is entirely coincidental.

Mentoris Project
745 South Sierra Madre Drive
San Marino, CA 91108

Cover photo: Photo 12 / Alamy Stock Photo

Cover design: Jim Villaflores

More information at www.mentorisproject.org

ISBN: 978-1-947431-46-1

Library of Congress Control Number: 2022936027

All net proceeds from the sale of this book will be donated to the Mentoris Project whose mission is to support educational initiatives that foster an appreciation of history and culture to encourage and inspire young people to create a stronger future.

Publisher's Cataloging-in-Publication (Provided by Cassidy Cataloguing Services, Inc.)

Names: Parker, W. A. W. (William Adam W.), author.
Title: The judicious use of intangibles : a novel based on the life of Pietro Belluschi / W.A.W. Parker.
Description: San Marino, CA : The Mentoris Project, [2022]
Identifiers: ISBN: 9781947431461 (paperback) | 9798201981044 (ebook) | LCCN: 2022936027
Subjects: LCSH: Belluschi, Pietro, 1899-1994--Fiction. | Architects--United States --History--20th century--Fiction. | Modern movement (Architecture)--Fiction. | Italian-Americans--History--20th century--Fiction. | LCGFT: Biographical fiction. | Historical fiction. | BISAC: FICTION / Biographical. | FICTION / Historical / General.
Classification: LCC: PS3616.A7515 J83 2022 | DDC: 813/.6--dc23

The Mentoris Project is a series of novels and biographies about the lives of great men and women who have changed history through their contributions as scientists, inventors, explorers, thinkers, and creators. The Barbera Foundation sponsors this series in the hope that, like a mentor, each book will inspire the reader to discover how she or he can make a positive contribution to society.

Contents

Foreword

First and foremost, Mentor was a person. We tend to think of the word *mentor* as a noun (a mentor) or a verb (to mentor), but there is a very human dimension embedded in the term. Mentor appears in Homer's *Odyssey* as the old friend entrusted to care for Odysseus's household and his son Telemachus during the Trojan War. When years pass and Telemachus sets out to search for his missing father, the goddess Athena assumes the form of Mentor to accompany him. The human being welcomes a human form for counsel. From its very origins, becoming a mentor is a transcendent act; it carries with it something of the holy.

The Mentoris Project sets out on an Athena-like mission: We hope the books that form this series will be an inspiration to all those who are seekers, to those of the twenty-first century who are on their own odysseys, trying to find enduring principles that will guide them to a spiritual home. The stories that comprise the series are all deeply human. These books dramatize the lives of great men and women whose stories bridge the ancient and the modern, taking many forms, just as Athena did, but always holding up a light for those living today.

Whether in novel form or traditional biography, these books

plumb the individual characters of our heroes' journeys. The power of storytelling has always been to envelop the reader in a vivid and continuous dream, and to forge a link with the subject. Our goal is for that link to guide the reader home with a new inspiration.

What is a mentor? A guide, a moral compass, an inspiration. A friend who points you toward true north. We hope that the Mentoris Project will become that friend, and it will help us all transcend our daily lives with something that can only be called holy.

—Robert J. Barbera, Founder, The Mentoris Project
—Ken LaZebnik, Founding Editor, The Mentoris Project

Chapter One

SUNRISE. SUNSET.

If you stand in this spot long enough, you can see the sun rise and set over water in both directions without moving an inch. Too bad Pietro doesn't want to stand still. But then again, what five-year-old does?

Pietro races to the top of the hill, up where the ground disappears and all that's left is sky. If he stretches his arms far enough apart, they'll become wings.

Out on the horizon, the sky merges with the sea. Pietro squints. *What lies beyond it?*

Pietro wants to float high above this peninsula set out in the Adriatic and soar across the sea to distant shores.

Sunrise. Sunset. Light lapping. Water wrapping. Day after day, the sun rises and sets on the cliffs of Ancona. Every day the ocean smashes into rock but never tears it apart. Every day Pietro spreads his arms, wishing they were wings. Or if not wings, then fins, so he could leap off the cliffs, dive into the depths, and swim. Or perhaps both. He could fly like a fish and bob like a bird.

Pietro doubles over. *How silly.* He can't be both. He has to decide—what will it be today: fly or float, soar or swim? Pietro looks at his hands. What will they be: feathers or fins? But they're clammy to the touch. He can't decide.

So his imagination pulls him underwater.

He gulps, wishes his lungs were gills.

The salt from the ocean wafts into the air, where it reaches Pietro's nostrils. The air next to the ocean always smells sharper than it does in the rest of the town. Perhaps it's because of the salt. Salt always makes things taste more alive. Salt is good, unless it's in a wound. Pietro has heard people say that.

The air in his lungs gives him life. He flops around like a fish out of water.

He'll be a fish—for today, at least. He bends his arms out in front of him, using his fins to push the water past his lungs.

The lungs are among the most important body parts, and the elbows are often the most overlooked. Pietro lives in the Elbow, or Ancona, Italy, as it's called. The town got its name from *ankón*, Greek for *elbow*. The arm bends at the elbow. And in Ancona, the land bends out into the ocean, forming a peninsula. The sun rises over the Adriatic and sets over the gulf.

Pietro splashes around the Ancona Cathedral, a Romanesque church atop the peninsula, standing guard over the sea. Pietro crests the waves in his imagination, taking another big swallow before diving below. Then his brow furrows. His lips smack of salt. He tastes the ocean, smells it. And there's another aroma. What could it be?

His eyes become saucers. *Mussels!* But then he furrows his brow. *What time is it? Where is the sun?*

Pietro centers himself on the church, spots the sun shining over Christ's cathedral, and uses the dome as a dial, marking the angle, even though it's no St. Mark's.

Pietro's mouth drops. Then he gasps for air, even though he's not a fish. If he doesn't get home in time for dinner soon, he might become it. It's not only time for dinner; it's time to run.

Pietro bounds down Via del Comune, down the hilly slope. Each step is carefully and quickly laid out, like a mountain goat's. Will he make it home in time? One can only hope.

Luckily, he lives only a short distance away. Close to his play. Pietro hurtles through the doorway and finds his family sitting around the table in their packed apartment. But Grandma hasn't placed the platter on the table. There's still time. Pietro launches himself into the open seat. No, not the one left vacant for his grandfather. That one stays empty. His grandfather was one of the railroad's first fatalities. It's an odd distinction, but then again, Pietro's family *is* odd.

His father, Guido, keeps a journal of every malady he's ever had, even skinned knees and sore throats, ever since he had yellow fever and smallpox as a child. Pietro's mother, Camilla, gives off the maternal energy of a viper. She fell ill soon after Pietro's birth and arranged for a live-in maid to care for her until she got her strength back. But she still hasn't recovered. She can't carry anything except for resentment.

If she could lift something, it would be a club. Camilla

never seems excited to have children unless she's ordering them around the apartment. Or listening to Margherita sing. Pietro's sister Margherita is only four years older than him but is already training to be an opera singer. To Pietro's young ears, though, it's less "training" and more "straining." Margherita can squelch out a decent *O Mio Babbino Caro*, a song about a young woman yearning for marriage, but who would want to marry Margherita after listening to her sing is anyone's guess.

Margherita is only nine, but Camilla is already planning her wedding. More importantly, she's planning her reception—not Margherita's, but Camilla's. After the wedding, Camilla will make her grand entrance back into society by singing the Queen of the Night aria from *The Magic Flute* to her daughter in front of everyone, even though the song choice may not be appropriate for the occasion.

Next to Margherita are Pietro's auntie and uncle. It can be both easy and odd to describe Pietro's relationship to them. He rarely likes to get into it, but while we're making introductions, let's try. His uncle is his father's brother, but he's also his aunt's husband. Similarly, his auntie is his mother's sister, but she's also his uncle's wife. But neither of them are "in-laws." No, that's still too confusing. Basically, Pietro's father's brother married Pietro's mother's sister. Two brothers married two sisters. And they all live together in one packed apartment. One big, happy family all packed together clammily.

At the head of the table, across from Grandfather's empty chair, sits Grandmother, a matriarch with spark, clearly showing who gave Camilla her bark. "Where's dinner?" she calls to Camilla in the kitchen.

Camilla's face sours as she adds lemon to the dish. She has her helper bring it to the table.

Grandmother leads them in saying grace before she takes a big scoop of pasta the size of her face. Together, Pietro's family eats *in grotta*, mussels caught off the rocks that day mixed with pasta, a favorite not only in their apartment but in all of Ancona.

Dinner, then mass—it's been the Belluschi family tradition every Saturday since Pietro can remember. Although he can't remember all that far back, actually, but it still seems like a long time to him.

Pietro drags his feet as they walk up the hill. He crosses to the other side of the street, cross with his family for dragging him to yet another mass, but they don't notice. There are so many of them, they take up almost the entire street anyway. It's not that Pietro hates going to mass. No, sometimes it can be a fun game to try to figure out what the priests are saying. Pietro hasn't started school. He hasn't learned a lick of Latin, so it's all Greek to him. Trying to decipher what's actually going on is the only game he can play during church. You can't spread your arms into wings, you can't turn them into fins. You can only stand there and listen, even before the priest begins.

You can't even sit; there are no pews. You can rent chairs, but the Belluschis don't. They attend church so often that the cost would quickly add up, and they can't afford the expense, even though Pietro's father has a good job as a minor official in the office of land assessment for the railroad. Pietro's grandfather worked for the railroad and so does his father. Working for the railroad is a Belluschi family tradition, just like eating *in grotta* and then marching to mass. Why should Pietro even think about going into any other profession? Why bother?

Pietro's grandmother, the most devout and stout of them all, says standing during the service builds character. Mussels are big in Ancona; they like them in their pasta and they like them in their legs. But she *would* say that. If Pietro knows anything about his grandmother, it's that she's his mother's mother. Sometimes Pietro thinks she enjoys watching him squirm, changing his weight from one foot to another, trying to hold firm. But Saturday mass is only a precursor to Sunday mass. And in both he's not allowed to squirm. And he's not allowed to sass.

Pietro loves cresting the hill to the cathedral to play on the peninsula, but sometimes he's too tired to do it. On this particular day, though, he learns something that gives him the energy to climb, maybe even all the way to the church's dome. Pietro's father is being transferred from Ancona to Rome.

It's 1905. And Pietro is now six. He's still a small fish, but he's already bristling at the size of his pond.

He was born in 1899, a century ago, and Ancona still feels stuck in the one before that.

Even though he'll only be traveling across land, Pietro leaps into the air. Anywhere is better, as long as it's out of Ancona. Anywhere as long as there's adventure.

He has so many questions about what he's about to

encounter, what he's about to do, but at the moment, Pietro's only concern is what happened on Saturday and Sunday, and all the Saturdays and Sundays before that. He's concerned about something much closer to home.

"Do the churches have seats in Rome?"

Chapter Two

THE TOMB

It looks like a plate trimmed with gold. Its edges are soft. The amber light refracts around a circle, creating a chasm into the clouds. Everything climaxes in that spot in the center, a dark circle surrounded by white, a pupil, almost as if God were looking back at you.

Pietro gazes into the frescoed cupola of *Sant'Agnese* in Rome. This church doesn't have pews either, but he's still mesmerized by the magnificent baroque design by Francesco Borromini.

The only place Pietro is allowed to sit is in school, but he fidgets as much there as he does in church. There's so much to learn outside the classroom, so why can't they have class outside? There's so much to see in Rome: St. Peter's. The Sistine Chapel. The Colosseum. The carriages. The washerwomen stringing up row after row of clothes in the street. Are there enough people for all these linens? There are so many people in Rome and everyone is walking somewhere. The city has an odd odor, one Pietro can't quite place yet. In Ancona, he could always tell how far he was from the sea by how much salt was in the air. Sometimes he could do it by sensing the incense wafting in and out of the cathedral, but here in Rome, there are so many of them. So many cathedrals. So many steeples. So many people. Perhaps the odd thing about the aroma of Rome is that there's not just one scent, but many on top of each other, all simmering together in a pot.

Pietro savors roaming about Rome, smelling the perfume of pots of pasta prepared in the kitchens he passes. His father loves the scent of the city too. The two take long walks together where Guido talks about his love of language, literature, and linguine.

Guido misses the mussels, but he muses about the Muses, the museums, and all the mausoleums they get to visit in their new home.

"What's your favorite part of Rome?" Guido asks his son.

As Pietro considers the question, his eyes wander. He looks past the remains of the Temple of Saturn toward the Temple of Antoninus and Faustina. Everything in the Forum smells like sod, like old earth. But maybe that's just the men digging into the ground a stone's throw away.

"I like it . . . here," Pietro responds.

"Ah, the Forum," Guido says, "where Rome lifts up her skirt and shows you what's underneath. Unlike all the other buildings throughout the city, it's only here where we didn't cover up the past."

Pietro smiles. He enjoys strolling around the Forum, but what he meant was: he likes it here, with his father.

"Is this place one of your muses, Pietro?" Guido asks, but doesn't wait for the answer. "You must find your muses. Or, perhaps, let them find you."

Guido enjoys telling Pietro all about his own muses, the books and songs and symphonies he's encountered in his life that have impacted him, the things he thinks about as he strolls or takes a bath or does anything worthwhile.

"I have my own muses, Pietro, and as much as I want to give mine to you, I know they'll mean more to you if they are your own, if they come from you and your experience."

Pietro rolls his eyes. His father is always saying things like this, especially when they go out for one of their long, meandering walks. Guido likes to turn them into long, meandering talks. Pietro loves his father, but sometimes, when he talks and talks, Pietro balks.

But there's nothing Pietro balks at more than helping his father and uncle build their new house. He loves spending time with his father, but he's too young to do anything useful, so it's a lot of standing around, more like church than construction.

Dust hovers in the air as Guido mixes the foundation.

"Every house must have a good foundation," Guido explains.

"Is there any part of the house that doesn't need to be?" Pietro wonders.

Guido scratches his head. "No, all of it needs to have at least some semblance of good."

Then, as if God wanted to drive the lesson home, a sinkhole opens up underneath Guido's feet and sucks him down into the ground!

"Father! Father? Are you all right?" Pietro calls down to him.

"Grab my journal!"

"Should I fetch a doctor?"

"My journal! Bring me my journal!"

Pietro looks around. *Where is it?* His father usually keeps it nearby. "Are you sure it didn't fall down too?" he asks.

Guido furrows his brow, then reaches underneath and pulls it out. "It must have broken my fall!"

Guido fishes out the pencil he stowed between pages, eager to scribble down his injury. He stands up gingerly. *Oof.* That ankle hurts. Guido's face contorts from pain to pleasure. First the pain of stepping on a sprained ankle, then the pleasure of writing it down for posterity.

"Are you all right?" Pietro asks.

"No! I got sucked into the ground! I could have died!"

Guido pats himself down. Checks for scrapes. But everything else seems in order, except for the ankle. He sighs, slightly disappointed.

"I'm sure I'll have some bruises tomorrow. Might need you to check my back for that."

Then Guido raises his head, no longer focused on his figure, but what's framing it. A small beam of light cascades into the space from above, bouncing off the stone below, illuminating the environs. Guido reaches down. This is no ordinary stone; it's smooth. Or at least parts of it are. A patchwork of odd-sized stones, almost like broken-up tiles, lines the floor. As his eyes adjust, Guido sees the space for what it is.

"Grab a ladder!"

Pietro lowers it into the sinkhole, holding the top, steadying it for his father's ascent.

"Are you going to come down here or what?" Guido asks incredulously.

"What do you mean—"

"Just get down here already!"

Pietro descends. His eyes adjust slowly. At first all he can decipher is . . . rust? The brown of the stone glows.

"What is it, Papà?"

"It's a catacomb."

Pietro cocks his head to the side. This is not a word Pietro has heard in school or on the street.

"You know what a church is, don't you?" Guido asks.

"So this is an underground church?"

"Well, not exactly. Not anymore. But can you imagine why someone might want to build a church underground?"

Pietro furrows his brow. He does it just like his father. What could it be? "Would they do it if they were hiding? But, Papà, why would anyone want to hide their church?"

"How many churches did you see in the Forum?" Guido asks.

"There was the Temple of Saturn and the Temple of Antoninus and Faustina and—"

"Yes, those are *temples*, Pietro. Temples to pagan gods. Did you see where the men were digging, though?"

"Yes, Papà."

"There they've rediscovered the Church of Santa Maria Antiqua. It might be the oldest church in the Forum. There aren't many churches in the Forum, although there is the San Sebastiano al Palatino and the Church of Saint Frances. There's also the Basilica of Saints Cosmas and Damian and, of course, the Church of Saint Joseph of the Carpenters, as well as a few churches on the outskirts of the—" Guido stops himself. "But the point is, there are a lot of temples there too, and it hasn't always been easy being a Christian, you know."

Pietro nods as if he does, but he searches his memory. Does he?

Guido catches his confusion. "You know we were persecuted, don't you?"

Pietro shakes his head. He's six. He hasn't quite conquered the history of interreligious warfare yet.

"Well, look around," Guido continues. "Look around at what we can do."

Pietro complies, spies a small space. It's much smaller than a church. In Ancona, and here in Rome too, hundreds of people sit in attendance during the service. But here, it looks like only a dozen congregants could congregate at any one time. The walls are rough, clearly carved by hand but never smoothed to the touch.

"We built places like this to escape persecution."

"What's persecution, Papà?"

"Some people didn't like us, so we built places like this so we could worship in peace."

Pietro spots a skeleton, swallows. "Were they murdered, Papà?"

"No, this is also a cemetery for our dead. I mean, some of them might have been murdered, but it might be a little hard to determine which of them died via natural causes and which were murdered and *then* dragged down here. The point is, they're dead. And how they died is irrelevant at the moment, because we need to figure out what we're going to do with them."

"Are we going to bury them?"

"Well, they're already buried. The problem is, they're right under our house and . . . I guess we could bury them even more, if you know what I mean."

Pietro nods, even though he doesn't.

"But first," Guido continues, "I think we should pray together."

Guido bends his knees, sucks in air. "Ooh, this is going to—" he starts to say, but he realizes his sprained ankle isn't smarting as much as it was before. "Oh, well, maybe it'll balloon up overnight."

Pietro joins his father on his knees and clasps his hands together.

"Please, Father, forgive us for our sins. Forgive us for what we must do. Forgive us . . ."

And that's when Pietro stops paying attention to his father's prayer. It's not that his father is prattling on; it's that Pietro perceives the power of prayer washing over him. He senses the prayers of his ancestors ricocheting around the catacomb, lashing around, yearning to be unleashed. Their earnest desires surge through him. The ecstasy of their worship beams out of his brain, up through the hole in the ground, directly to God himself.

"Amen," his father ends.

"Amen," Pietro repeats. He blinks and looks around. He's back in the catacomb. "But . . . what must we do, Papà?"

"Sometimes you can't hold on to the past," Guido explains. "Sometimes, like with our house, you have to build something new for the future. *Our* future."

Pietro nods. He understands. You can't always hold on to the past. There's a time and place to remember it, like at the Forum. But if Rome treated its past like it did the Forum, there would be no Rome, only Forum. There'd be no place for new buildings. No place to build the Belluschi home.

Guido stands up. Pietro follows, grabbing a hand to stand. But it's not his father's hand. Guido is already over by the ladder. Whose hand is he grabbing? Slowly, Pietro turns to his side, finding the bones of a dismembered hand in his.

Pietro screams as the bones dissolve to powder. The skeleton sifts through his fingers like sand in an hourglass.

He bolts to his feet, flails, and rubs the remains on his shirt. Then he realizes what he's done and rips it off.

No, you can't hold on to the past. But then again, why would you?

Chapter Three

MOZART & SALIERI

An old man's lament. The pain reverberates in his throat. And why wouldn't it? Death surrounds him. It's toying with him.

Pietro watches the old man sing his sorrow. The man is Antonio Salieri. Or at least that's who the actor is portraying. He has lines painted on his face instead of wrinkles, and his voice has more gusto than bravado. The actor doesn't possess the timbre of an older man, but he has the ferocious will of one, especially one who's been wronged.

Pietro's father has taken him to see his sister Margherita perform in Nikolai Rimsky-Korsakov's opera *Mozart and Salieri.* It's an adaption of Alexander Pushkin's 1830 drama of the same name, but more importantly, it's Margherita's debut.

Unfortunately, like Salieri, she's not content about her place in it either. Over the course of Pietro's childhood, Margherita droned on and on about her desire to be an opera singer, how she would execute the most difficult arias flawlessly, but in her debut she doesn't get to sing a single note. *Mozart and Salieri* doesn't have singing roles for anyone outside the titular characters. Margherita plays the blind fiddler who enters during the middle of act one, plays a quick violin solo, then exits the stage for the rest of the show. In this relative two-hander, it's a breath of fresh air that turns out to be a discordant note. The director said he thought of Margherita for the role after he heard her singing in another audition.

Like the actor playing Salieri, Margherita has to pretend to be older than she is, wrinkles painted on her face. Her hair is pulled back so tight she looks like a man, the type of old, blind fiddler you'd find on any popular thoroughfare. In essence, she looks the part.

Pietro wishes he were an older man. He's thirteen. Such a strange age. Finally, a teenager. No longer a child, but not yet a man. No, he has a few more years before that occurs. His mother likes to remind him of that. If his family were Jewish, he'd be a man by now, at least technically. Pietro would consider converting, but he'd have to convince the entire family, and they wouldn't have that.

His mother made sure to send him to the opera wearing a jacket and tie. She was much too sickly to go herself. She's always too sickly to go anywhere.

Pietro wishes he looked more macho. Margherita looks more masculine in her fiddler's getup than he does in his jacket. But the two of them are only playing at being a man, whereas Antonio Salieri is showing them how to be one.

Pietro can't quite figure out what's going on in the opera. Pietro senses Salieri isn't spellbound being the second fiddle in this two-hander. He's older than Mozart, who isn't sporting any pencil-wrinkles on his face and is decidedly less carefree, but Pietro can tell Salieri is jealous of Mozart.

Pietro only discerned the man was Salieri, though, after the older actor sang a word Pietro recognized. Everything else sounded garbled, but this word came out clear as a bell: *Mozart*. Then Pietro connected the dots when Mozart, a younger, preening gentleman, pranced onto the stage.

Pietro can't understand what's going on because the opera is Russian, although he's heard several Italian operas too, and even then the singers wrapped their mouths around the words so tightly that they strangled any understanding. Then again, maybe opera isn't entirely dependent on words. Perhaps it's more about emotion. If that's the case, Pietro understands what's going on well enough.

It helps that Pietro knows a bit about Mozart. He's heard a few things here and there. He knows that by the time Mozart was thirteen, he'd already written several symphonies and operas. Mozart spent his childhood parading around the courts of Europe, playing for kings and queens. Some say he was more like a dancing monkey. An overtrained monkey who danced his fingers upon the keys of a piano. That's how the younger actor is portraying him. Mozart prances across the stage as he sings, running rings around Salieri.

When Mozart leaves, Pietro can see the pain in Salieri's face. But he isn't sad Mozart left. Rather, Salieri reveals the emotions he was hiding from the younger man all along. There's a yearning. Perhaps a plan?

When the second scene starts, Salieri seems resolved. Mozart mentions his Requiem. That's a word Pietro knows. Mozart is no longer prancing. He must be telling Salieri a serious story.

Salieri pours Mozart a drink. Maybe to end his nerves? Mozart gulps it down, but Salieri doesn't. Usually, one drink cheers a man up and many drinks make him sad. Salieri seems sad, even though he hasn't drunk anything. Perhaps he had a few between scenes. Or maybe he put something in Mozart's drink?

Before, Salieri held up a small vial. Whatever liquid was in the vial, it didn't compare to the vile emotion Salieri seemed to have about it. He was determined, but now, after Mozart drinks the wine Salieri supplied him, Salieri looks like the ghost Mozart might soon be.

Did Salieri poison Mozart, jealous of the young man's fame? It seems to be the dramatic question at hand. Pietro's chest hitches. He can tell from the look on Salieri's face that he poisoned Mozart. But the maestro doesn't know it yet. Mozart is not in a panic. He's in a cage but is not yet cagey, his ignorance giving him this moment of bliss before he's taken down in the abyss. Mozart is being murdered, but he's not dead yet. He's in that medium state, the one embodied in his Requiem, the one that plays the death toll that now rings for him. Mozart extends his arms, conducting his own mass. His somber notes take over the musical reigns from Rimsky-Korsakov.

When Mozart finishes, his face goes slack. Is he dead? Alive? Either way, he's at peace. The audience erupts into applause even though, as Pietro will soon learn, the opera isn't over. But

Mozart's Requiem is finished, and his applause will not wait for another composer.

Then Salieri launches into his own requiem. He crescendos with all the pain in his soul. All his demons dance out of his mouth. It's a dying wish, but it's not fulfilled. When Salieri collapses, it's Mozart's music that reigns over his body. It's Mozart's music that lifts Salieri up, taking him into the heavens. Or so Pietro envisions when he closes his eyes.

When he opens them, he finds Mozart's arms outstretched, welcoming Salieri. But is Mozart an angel, a devil? Christ himself on the cross? Or is he just conducting? Either way, his arms are open. His chest is unprotected. He's vulnerable. You can do anything you want to him. Treat him any way you like.

That's what Rimsky-Korsakov and Pushkin have done. The story was mesmerizing, but Pietro can't help but wonder whether the lives of these two men might have been more complicated than this simple story allowed. Pietro smiles. It's a grown-up thought. Perhaps he's more of a man than his mother thinks he is.

As the curtain falls and Margherita takes her bow, Pietro furrows his brow. He has another grown-up thought: After he's a man, once he grows up and does something on par with Mozart or, heaven forbid, Salieri, will his family see him as more than a man? And once he's dead, will anyone else do the same? Rimsky-Korsakov and Pushkin did it with Salieri in the opera. From what he can gather, Pietro surmises they turned Salieri into more than a composer. They turned him into an idea.

Before now, Pietro had never heard of Salieri. But he had heard of Mozart. Pietro could walk up to anyone on the street and they could tell him Mozart was a visionary genius. So, given what he's seen, given the idea of a man Rimsky-Korsakov presents, was Salieri only able to bask in Mozart's brilliance, having none of his own? Did he really have a part to play in Mozart's death?

Pietro has so many questions for Margherita after she removes her makeup, after she removes the pencil-wrinkles from her face. But she doesn't seem to be able to remove all the wrinkles. Or more precisely, this experience has given her some. And she doesn't want to answer any of Pietro's questions.

"I'm done trying to be an opera singer," she says sullenly.

Apparently, there were three deaths onstage that night: Mozart, Salieri, and Margherita's career. And she was true to her word. Margherita never took another singing lesson. Soon after her debut, which turned out to be her finale, Margherita met an engineer and engineered a proposal out of him.

Margherita appears manifestly feminine on her wedding day, a stark contrast to her fiddler's garb. No, no one could mistake Margherita for a man today. She's a vision in white, but Pietro can only think about the opera. He hasn't been able to think about much else lately. Pietro's been having trouble paying attention in school too, because his mind is always focused on what he's learning outside it. Because Margherita was no help with his queries after the performance, Pietro has used his breaks at school to retreat into the library and research the lives of Mozart and Salieri. Pietro has learned that Mozart, while brilliant, was bred for success, given every opportunity. Mozart had issues with his father, but Salieri had to overcome not having one. Both of Salieri's parents died in his early teens. He didn't have anyone pushing him; he had to push himself. Mozart was born into success, but Salieri had to make himself into one. And there's no real historical evidence to suggest Salieri had any part in Mozart's death.

It confirms Pietro's gut reaction that maybe Rimsky-Korsakov was making Salieri into more of an idea than a man. On its face, the opera is a made-up story full of made-up facts. But it seemed real. And Salieri made a compelling choice in it. A complicated choice. Pietro has heard stories like this before in church. They're called parables. The story can be shallow, but the emotional and philosophical weight of the character's choice runs deep. Sometimes there is no correct choice, only the one made in the moment.

In the opera it was clear who he should root for, but based on reality, Pietro isn't so sure. Who should he root for: the lauded genius or the man who worked his way up from obscurity? Who should Pietro try to emulate? Whose example should he follow?

Pietro will need more than a moment to think about it.

Chapter Four

THE FUTURIST MANIFESTO

Plumes of sawdust. As soon as someone sits, they wish they hadn't. There's no getting comfortable in these chairs. When someone plops down, powdery particles fly into the air, leading to nothing but itchy eyes and despair.

Pietro waves his hand in front of his face, weaving through the plumes and fumes of sawdust. He's glad his father isn't with him tonight. Guido would document his encounter with sawdust, and it would make Pietro blush. His father can be so embarrassing sometimes, but . . . Guido is his father, and at the end of the day his father lets him explore Rome on his own. Pietro has taken to calling him Guido sometimes, instead of Father or Papà. Guido doesn't like it, but then again, Guido doesn't like a lot of things.

Pietro fell in love with the theatre back when he and Guido went to see *Mozart and Salieri,* but his father took Margherita's finale as an opportunity to take his exit as well. While Guido likes books, he doesn't much care for theatre folk.

"They're crooks," Guido likes to say before Pietro pops out

for a night of theatre. Pietro is fifteen now. He's old enough to attend the theatre on his own. Or at least that's what his parents say when they don't want to go with him.

Tonight, Pietro is on his way to see a series of short plays. *Serates*, they're called. If only he could make his way to his seat. A group of men are blocking the aisle.

"No, this is my seat. I have the ticket right here," one man says.

"I don't care what your ticket says! It's mine and I was here first!" another yells as he crosses his arms and stays seated. The group of men all wave their tickets at each other. Then they swap out the tickets for their own faces, squawking and screaming at each other with almost no room for the sawdust to fly between them.

Pietro picks up a couple tickets that dropped to the floor. He squints at them. Are they all . . . the same? The tickets are duplicates of each other. Identical row, identical seat. And the men are very similar too. All of them are big, burly men. Not quite the theatre type, but men of a more masculine stripe.

"Gentlemen, I think it's clear what happened," Pietro attempts to announce. "You were sold the same ticket. All of you."

But the men aren't interested in Pietro's realization. Two of them try to lift the sitting man out of his seat. Then the sitting man swings, which sets off a series of swipes, and the men devolve into a massive melee.

A tornado of dust sweeps through the audience. People hack

and cough. Pietro sneezes, wheezes, looks at the men like they're diseases.

Luckily, a man in a bow tie enters stage left. His stride is sure, purposeful. He knows how to put things right.

"Fight!" he screams, then shoots a pistol. *Bang!*

The men stop. Others plop into their seats. And some run out of the theatre. But the man mesmerizes Pietro. Pietro can't go; he stands there, his hand outstretched like Mozart's. But rather than being at the end of his life, the man has something in his hand to take someone else's. Thankfully, it doesn't look like he's going to. The man stands there, still, leaving everyone to wonder if he's going to cause ill.

The man isn't smiling, but his moustache is, the corners twisted up into a curl on the sides.

"That was my first performance. Titled *Detonation*," he says grandly. "I call the next one *Electric Dolls* because it features a lovely, bourgeois couple and their lovely, bourgeois robots. Although," the man pauses for dramatic effect, "is it the couple who owns the robots, or do the robots own them?"

Pietro widens his eyes, even though the sawdust irritates them. He dashes over to his seat and stays glued to it for the rest of the performance. He's heard that the man on stage, this Marinetti, the man who wrote the play, likes to play with his audience, but Pietro didn't imagine it would be anything like this.

Pietro replays the events preceding the *Detonation*. His mind explodes. Was that a part of the performance as well? How about the sawdust? Are these questions Pietro's having . . . also part of the experience? Is Marinetti making a play in Pietro's mind in addition to the one onstage? Either way, it's making it difficult for Pietro to pay attention to the performance. His mind cycles through these questions until Marinetti takes center stage and fires off another shot. No, he doesn't fire a gun; he does something much more fun.

Filippo Tommaso Marinetti pulls out a parchment and proceeds to read his *Futurist Manifesto,* stopping the play cold. Some members of the audience walk out. But they don't do so quietly; they shout.

"What a bunch of nonsense!"

"No wonder it was a free ticket!"

"I know a better use for that gun!"

But Marinetti stands strong, proceeding with his screed: "Our hearts filled with an immense pride. We stood alone, like lighthouses or sentinels in an outpost . . ."

Marinetti is the lighthouse, shining his light, Pietro thinks, mixing his internal monologue with Marinetti's.

"At last, mythology has been left behind. The mystic cult of the ideal . . . left behind."

There is no place for that way of thinking anymore.

"We dictated our first will and testament to all the living men on Earth. One! We want to sing the love of danger, the habit of energy and rashness. Two! The essential elements of our poetry will be courage, audacity, and revolt. Three! Literature has up to now magnified pensive immobility, ecstasy, and slumber.

We want to exalt movements of aggression, feverish sleeplessness, the double march, the perilous leap, the slap, and the blow with the fist."

Break it up. Use your fists if you must. Sometimes the only way to get someone's attention is with a gun.

"Nine! We want to glorify war. It is the only cure for the world. Militarism, patriotism, the destructive gesture of the anarchists, the beautiful ideas which kill, and contempt for woman. Ten! We want to demolish museums and libraries, fight the so-called morality, feminism, and all opportunist and utilitarian cowardice."

This is where Pietro's mind wanders back to his own—or at least to his stomach. Pietro's thoughts had been so entwined with Marinetti's, his passion, his rhetoric. But now, Pietro believes he's going to be sick. He wants to throw up, but finds he's glued to his seat. The spell is broken, but the glue is holding firm.

The audience boos its displeasure. They've had enough. A cavalcade parades out, and the rest squirm in their seats similar to Pietro. It appears that, in addition to the sawdust, Marinetti placed glue on a few chairs in the audience, trying to make sure at least some of them would stay for the entire performance.

Two of the burly men who bought the same ticket storm the stage.

"Look what you did to my britches!" one yells.

"You sold the same ticket to me and all these others sons of—" the other man hollers as they chase him out of the theatre, hot on his collar.

Pietro can only pry himself free when he leaves a small patch of his pants behind, a small swatch now permanently part of the theatre.

Pietro runs after Marinetti as well, but he doesn't want to yell. He wants to talk, hear more, hear what else Marinetti had in store.

When Pietro makes it to the stage door, he sees the burly men rounding a corner.

"Psst! Over here! Is the coast clear?" Marinetti peaks out from behind a pile of rubbish, apparently not taking any potential harassment from this scrawny fifteen-year-old too seriously.

Pietro whips around, waits a moment. Footsteps stomp in the distance, but there are no storms of sawdust, no tornadoes headed their way.

"It's just us," Pietro says.

Marinetti shuffles off the detritus from his suit. He starts down the alleyway in the direction opposite the men after him. Pietro wants to stop him. He wants to ask Marinetti so many questions. Did he really sell all those men the same ticket?

But all he can muster is, "Why?"

It was all he needed to ask. Marinetti stops in his tracks, looks back. He squints at Pietro, almost as if he's asking himself, *Is this young man worth my time?*

Pietro takes his pause as an opportunity to elaborate. "Why the glue? Why the gun? Why the sawdust? Why any of it?"

"In there?" Marinetti chuckles. "You mean, why did I do things like sell all those men the same ticket? Perhaps you should ask yourself, why were all of them . . . men? And why did they become so angry? Why was it so easy to find men to do exactly what I wanted them to do? *Detonation* was not the first performance. *They* were. And they performed it spectacularly."

Now it's time for Pietro to squint, but he's not sizing Marinetti up; he's considering what he just said.

Marinetti points right at Pietro's brain. "That right there, what you're thinking, that's part of my performance too. It is the duty of an artist—it is my duty—not to entertain an audience, but to get them to think. To find fresh forms, share unique visions of the world, even if they are wrong."

"But who's to say what's wrong and what's right?" Pietro asks him.

"Precisely," Marinetti says. "Do you take your direction from an artist, or is it from someplace deep inside you?"

Pietro nods along. There's nothing more intoxicating to a teenager than new ideas, especially if they upend the traditional functioning of society.

"I want to do something new too. Something different," Pietro says, the words emptying out of him as soon as they enter his brain. "But when does your performance in my brain stop? And when does my own thinking come back into it again? Maybe I could make something about that."

"Don't be derivative," Marinetti says derisively.

"No. No, of course not," Pietro apologizes. "But I promise you I am going to do something, something to really shake things up, contribute to society."

Marinetti smirks, looks down the street. "Yeah, and what'll that be?"

Pietro shrugs. He's not quite sure, but there is one thing he's sure of. He looks at Marinetti square in the eye. "I'll let you know as soon as I figure that out."

Chapter Five

THE GREAT WAR

Four o'clock in the morning. Not three o'clock. Three o'clock at night is exactly that: at night. Four o'clock is the earliest you can rise and have it be the start of a new day. And that's precisely when Pietro awakens. Today and every day for the past few months.

Many men were drafted into the Great War, but the real men enlisted. Or at least that's what the recruiter tells Pietro. But Pietro doesn't need to be convinced. He joins willingly. Enlists enthusiastically. This war will be Great, and Pietro wants to be a part of that greatness. Wars make men. They give them the opportunity to rise above their station.

Pietro wants to be an officer, and the only way he can do that, especially this late in the geopolitical game, is by enlisting. The war erupted in 1914. Italy joined the fray in 1915, after breaking off its Triple Alliance with Germany and Austria-Hungary. Then Italy joined forces with Britain, France, and the other Allied powers instead. So, Pietro has been preparing for this moment for the past two years.

"I'd like to enlist. I want to be an officer," Pietro spits out excitedly.

"How old are you?" the recruiter asks suspiciously.

"Seventeen today, sir."

"Ah, so you're still squeaky, aren't you?"

"I'm as ready as any man."

The recruiter laughs. "If you're still comparing yourself to a man, then you aren't one yet. Do you even have your high school diploma?"

High school diploma? Pietro needs to learn trigonometry in order to learn how to pull a trigger? Until now, Pietro has seen little benefit to paying attention in high school, but now it's time for him to learn his lesson.

"You'll need that if you want to be an officer," the recruiter explains.

Four years of goofing off in school. Four years of not paying attention. And it's all led here: four o'clock in the morning. That's the time Pietro has to wake up every day to study for his diploma. He marches all day in the army. Just because he lacks a diploma doesn't mean they wouldn't take him, but it does mean they won't send him to officer training until he has that piece of paper. The only time Pietro has to study is in the hour or two before he starts drills, and then whatever hours he has in the evening, assuming he's not too tired.

Cramming a high school education into the early morning hours for months on end is less painful than paying attention all those years, Pietro thinks, because now he's working toward something instead of trying to get out of it.

Early morning light. And then late into the night. Studying hard. His sight set on a gunfight.

Pietro has seen his name written many times before, but none of them can compare to the moment he sees his name on his high school diploma.

Pietro leaps from cobblestone to cobblestone as if they were rocks on a river, holding the diploma over his head like a child tugging on a kite. But Pietro is no child, although he waves the diploma in front of his commanding officer's face when he arrives back to the barracks.

"That's not a white flag you're waving, is it?" his commander jokes.

"No, it's . . . it's my . . ." Pietro stumbles. He's not stuttering, and he knows the name for the paper in his hand. That word just doesn't quite describe what it is exactly, or at least what it means to him. "It's my ticket out of here."

Pietro knows a thing or two about tickets. His father and his grandfather before him worked for the railroad. And this is his ticket away from that life. It's ironic, though, that the ticket away from his family's legacy still involves a train.

The train to Turin for officer training takes Pietro through the mountains—or, more appropriately, the hills on the way to the mountains. Turin is on the edge of the Alps, but when Pietro arrives, he discovers it's the city on the edge of many things. The most pressing at the time of his arrival is a labor strike.

"Grab a baton and come with us," Pietro is ordered when he shows up to officer training.

Pietro does what he's told. He's a good soldier, but he has a hard time keeping up with the other soldiers as they make their way through the narrow city streets.

He catches his breath when they stop in front of a factory. Outside, workers slowly mill about in a circle. They're performing their own sort of march, their own sort of formation. And they might as well, because the military has been treating them like soldiers. Many of the factories increased their output for the war, but wages hadn't always kept pace. And soldiers weren't the only ones finding themselves under military control. If a worker was absent from a factory, they were accused of the crime of desertion, just as if they were a soldier. Anyone who complained or had the audacity to mention a strike was sent to military tribunals instead of civil court. That's why all these workers are striking.

Pietro and the other soldiers form a line next to the strikers. Pietro turns right. Then left. A few of his future classmates caress their clubs a little too keenly.

"What are we here to do?" Pietro asks the cadet to his left.

"I think . . . this is it," he says cautiously. "Yesterday, all we did was this."

Pietro exhales. He wants to go to war, but not with his own people.

"How long do we do this?" Pietro follows up.

"I don't know. I've been here a week and this is all we've done."

And that's all they have Pietro do for a week. And another week. And the one after that. Pietro finds himself in the precarious position of overseeing the strikers instead of learning how to lead men into war. He receives only half the officer training they promised, but that doesn't stop the army from advancing him. What can they do, though? There's a war on and they need men. If only high school had been as easy as officer training.

And then they send Pietro from one mountain to another. He treks from the western edge of the Alps, near France, to the eastern side, near the action.

"Grab your gun and come with us," Pietro is ordered when he arrives at the front.

Pietro's entrée to the battlefield has a stunning similarity to his arrival at officer training, but he soon learns this will not be a repeat of that experience. There's no time for standing on the front lines, especially on this battlefield. The Italian army desperately needs officers. Italian Chief of Staff Luigi Cadorna fired 217 generals and 255 colonels for what he deemed their "lack of offensive spirit" after eleven unsuccessful campaigns in the Battles of the Isonzo River. Over a million men were casualties in these fights alone, six hundred and forty-five thousand on the Italian side. And Luigi was desperate to have more fodder for the cannons. Whether that fodder be for the Italian or Austrian cannons, though, is one of those details that often gets lost in war.

Pietro is lost. He pulls his mask over his face. Poison gas surrounds him. Everyone else disappears. He wades through the clouds. It's oddly calm. Oddly serene. It's almost as if he's a bird flying through the clouds, high in the air. But in this cloud there are too many monsters lingering just out of sight for it to be peaceful.

The Austrian artillery has been bombarding them with shells

for two hours and now they've switched to gas. Pietro tenses, knowing it's a precursor to their advance. Eleven Battles of the Isonzo, all Italian offenses near the town of Caporetto—or Kobarid, as the Slovenians call it—and now Pietro is plopped right in the thick of the Austrians' first offensive counterstrike.

Whoosh. A man runs past Pietro. *Bang!* Pietro learns why he's running.

"Retreat! Retreat!" The man screams.

Masses of men rush by Pietro, their ghostly figures barely registering in his corneas, although their stampede thunders in his ears.

Pietro turns to join the retreat, but the pop of a pistol pierces his periphery.

He tries to launch himself into a gallop, but he can hardly move. Pietro looks down. His leg is caught on something, but what? A flash of red seeps through his mask. He sees blood. *His* blood. Pietro's leg isn't caught; he's been shot.

A man who must be Austrian tackles Pietro, sending his gas mask flying. Pietro scrambles as the man jumps onto his back. He twists his body, bucking the man off.

Pietro scans the ground for his gun, but it must have disappeared into one of the clouds. The Austrian lunges at Pietro with his bayonet. Pietro tries to block it with his arm, but his arm isn't a shield. The blade rips through his flesh.

Pietro screams out, but pushes the Austrian back on his heels. He rips the Austrian's gun out of his hands, flips it around, and points it back at him.

Click. Pietro pulls the trigger, but the cartridge is spent. No bullet.

Smash. The Austrian tackles Pietro again. They crash to the ground. Pietro reaches around for the bayonet . . . and finds a rock instead.

Crack. Smack. Whack.

Pietro sees red again, but this time it's another man's blood. The Austrian's blood stains the ground, although with the yellow of the gas, it has an orange hue.

Almost sixty thousand Italian soldiers are being taken prisoner in the clouds surrounding Pietro, but he won't be one of them. Pietro limps away from the gunshots, slowly, methodically taking steps, climbing over the men who haven't been as lucky as him.

Pietro pushes himself forward, one foot in front of the other. Then lights flash around him. But they're not flashlights, just small squiggles wiggling about.

He can't quite tell where they're coming from. But there are no lights; it's just Pietro passing out. He scans the trail of blood he's leaving behind, a train of blood, like *Lucia di Lammermoor* on her wedding day.

Pietro throws himself down in front of a cross. A red cross. On the side of a truck.

"We've got one more!" a man around Pietro's age says as he rushes to his side.

"There's no more room!" another man calls out.

"Then help me get him in the cab!"

Together, the two angels lift Pietro off the ground and place him in the truck's passenger seat.

Pietro weaves in and out of consciousness as the driver weaves in and out of God knows what. Pietro's body sways around the cabin, but it's not enough to keep him awake.

"You can't go to sleep," the driver scolds.

But Pietro can't keep his eyes open. Maybe if he closes them, wraps his eyelids around his eyes tight, he can warm them up and escape this sensation, this cold.

Chapter Six

MAN PLAGUED THE WORLD, SO THE WORLD PLAGUED MAN

Dreaming. Sleeping. The great beyond is creeping. So many great men have been called to the great beyond in the Great War. Pietro senses them caressing him, hugging him, comforting him with their embrace. His eyelids are boulders shuttering him in his tomb. The arms pulling him down are warm. He's a baby in the womb. He's come full circle. There's no doom and gloom, just a sweet smell, a perfume.

It would be so easy to give in to the sensation surrounding him.

The driver slams on the gas and recites:

"*Once, if I recall correctly, my life was a banquet.*
The wine flowed. All hearts were open.
One night Beauty sat on my knee. I
found her bitter and I insulted her.
I armed myself against Justice.
I fled. You sorceress. You misery. And hatred.
I placed my treasure in your hands.

I succeeded in driving all hope from my mind. With the
stealth of beasts I leapt on every happiness and rung its neck.
I summoned executioners so I could bite on
the butts of their rifles in my death throes.
I invoked plagues to choke myself on the sand. On blood.
Despair has been my God. I've laid head to toe in the mud. I've
dried out in the crime-ridden air. I've run rings around madness.
And spring has brought me the hideous laugh of the idiot.
But lately, nearing the edge of uttering my last
squawk, I thought of searching for that key in that long-
gone banquet. Maybe my appetite would be restored.
The key is charity, which only proves
how deeply I've been dreaming."

Last squawk? Pietro balks. He doesn't understand English, but there's something in the rhythm of these words that captures his attention. He bolts upright. "What? What are you saying?"

"Thought I lost you there for a minute," the driver responds in Italian.

"Was . . . What was that?"

"Ah, you don't know Rimbaud?"

Rimbaud . . . Rimbaud . . . The name sounds oddly familiar, but Pietro searches his memory and comes up short. "No."

"No? No!" the driver escalates. "A young man like you out in the world doesn't know Rimbaud?"

"Who is he?"

"I just told you."

"No, you didn't. You—"

"I showed you. That's the same thing."

The driver had disgorged a lot of words and a name. It was less of an explanation and more of a game.

"Is this a game? Are you making fun of me?" Pietro asks.

"Ah, no. That would be lame." The driver clocks Pietro's leg wound. "Sorry, that might have been a poor choice of words. Given, you know . . . you might lose your leg."

Pietro's face turns white. The blood rushes out of his face, gushes out of his leg. But when Pietro checks his thigh, he finds it bandaged. The blood has stopped flowing, but the pain is growing.

"Will I be able to keep it?" Pietro asks earnestly.

"Who needs a leg when you have a peg?" the driver jokes.

Pietro freezes, the cold creeping into his veins.

"Sorry," the driver apologizes. "That little rhyme was just lying there. I had to scoop it up, much like I did with you. You'll be fine. Now that you're awake, that is. Who knew you'd respond so well to Rimbaud?" he asks, then answers his own question. "Me, I guess."

"And who exactly is Rimbaud?"

"Didn't I . . . ? He's . . . Well, he's the man who saved your life, is who he is. I tried out a few other poets before I got to him and you didn't budge an inch. So in that way, you could call him a sorcerer. He conjures worlds with his words. And apparently he can bring back people from the dead. Makes sense with how he lived. By the time he was eighteen, like me, he'd already traveled around Europe, raising Cain and leaving his stain, his mark, wherever he went."

"There's a big difference between a stain and a mark," Pietro says.

"Good sense might tell you that, but histories aren't written about people with good sense."

"Is that why you drive an ambulance instead of fighting?"

The driver wiggles his eyebrows, not taking the bait. "I thought about joining the army, but America wasn't in the fight yet, and the Red Cross said driving a truck is a special skill. But it's not my only one. I'm a writer."

"What have you written?"

"Working on something about the war right now. You'll hear about it when it comes out." The driver winks. "Ernest Hemingway. Remember the name."

The ambulance pulls up to an expansive makeshift hospital.

"And to answer your question before: Yes, this has been a game. The game is . . . keep you awake until we reach the hospital. And then I get to absolve myself of any responsibility about your well-being. Now, can you get out on your own or do I have to carry you?"

Pietro narrows his eyes. He doesn't know if this man has any future as a writer, but he might have one as a magician. Pietro's leg throbs. He didn't notice until now. But now that he does, the pain compounds, the delayed agony knowing no bounds.

Four o'clock in the morning. It's the time of day Pietro used to wake up to become a soldier. And now it's the time he wakes up every day to face the consequences of becoming one. The pain is his alarm clock.

All that work to become an officer, and now he's injured. This is not the greatness Pietro came to collect. This is not what he came here to do.

Pietro convalesces quickly. Time flies when you're hypnotized. Rimbaud's words fly around Pietro's skull: "Summoned executioners . . . Invoked plagues . . . Despair has been my God."

They're the words of a haunted man, not a vaunted one. Pietro senses the ghosts surrounding him even when he rejoins his fellow soldiers and leads them to victory at the Battle of the Piave River. It was a turning point, not just in the war, but in Pietro's perception of it. Victory can do that to a man. You achieve exactly what you wanted, then realize what you wanted isn't exactly what you need. What you need can be more illusory, more ephemeral, more like a ghost.

Perhaps that's what Rimbaud was trying to get at. This war. This Great War. Man is plaguing the world. So, in retaliation, the world plagues man.

Once the war was over, once Pietro helped end it, after he thought he had survived death, death decided it wasn't done.

The Spanish influenza epidemic rips across Europe with more ferocity than any army. And it does not tire. It does not get shot. And it doesn't need a gun to kill. It doesn't need to recuperate. The epidemic is Mozart to the Great War's Salieri. It runs rings around man.

Man thought he could conquer the world, but that's not how things unfurled.

Pietro thought he would travel the world after the war. He thought he would be like Rimbaud, leaving his mark. But the stain of the war lingers on every surface, infecting everyone it comes into contact with.

Pietro hides from this deadly enemy in his childhood bedroom.

"I've run rings around madness . . . I've run rings around madness . . ." The words whirl around Pietro's imagination during quarantine in Rome. His bedroom walls echo his pain back at him. His leg has long since healed, but the wounds in his brain have wormed their way in and become infected. He needs to talk to someone, but his parents locked themselves away in separate bedrooms, in their own little worlds, in their own little bubbles, fighting their own little wars. Talking to anyone, interacting with anyone, is too much trouble, too much of a risk. Too much a chance to make them sick. Pietro's father itches and aches, not from influenza, but to enter any tiny symptom he encounters into his journal. His mother cuts out all interaction altogether, even through a door, except for the woman she still hires to dote on her.

All Pietro has are the words of a madman to keep him company. Rimbaud's siren song cycles through his system, running rings around his madness. How long could you be cooped up during an epidemic? Afraid to find out? Chicken? Chickens often come to love their coops. It keeps the fox out.

But what happens when the fox strolls inside? What happens when the fox is in your mind?

Pietro needs to process his trauma, but he's locked inside. He can't do the things he needs to move forward. Both he and the world are at a standstill.

Words. There are too many words in Pietro's head. He needs to concentrate on something else instead. He picks up a pencil. And draws a man. He's dead, the man. You might not know by looking at him, but Pietro can tell, knows it to be true. But how can he show you? Maybe if the man were blue . . .

Pietro searches his room. What's blue? Blue is an uncommon color in nature, but it happens to be the hue of one of its most oddly named flowers: the forget-me-not. How could Pietro forget the forget-me-not? The blue of the sky seeps into its petals. The resplendent sun saturates its yellow center.

Once Pietro makes the man blue, once he makes it clear he's dead, Pietro gets another thought in his head: What if he drew a forget-me-not?

Pietro sketches the flower. His fingers flick. The entire process is quite quick. Pietro detects a surge, a sort of urge—to continue, to see what else is on the menu. What else could he draw?

Long days of drawing sprout into long nights. Pietro does everything he can to keep drawing, anything to keep the ghosts away, anything to keep away their frights.

When the quarantine ends and everything returns to normal, Pietro discovers he doesn't want to return to the world as it was. The world has changed, molded itself into a new form.

And Pietro wants to have that same power over himself. What is he going to do to achieve that, though? Don't worry, I'll tell you as soon as he knows.

Chapter Seven

AN ACCELERATED COURSE OF STUDY

There is no sweeter scent than freedom. Even the Forum's old earth smells like new sod. Pietro grins, gleeful to be out of the house, but he's even more gratified to have found an opportunity to keep drawing.

He plops on a rock and opens a notebook. Which building to draw? He needs to choose one in the Forum for class. *Class?* Pietro never thought he'd take another class. He finished high school, but only because he needed to become an officer.

Sometimes when an opportunity presents itself, though, you'd be a fool not to take it. And Pietro doesn't want to be a fool. But this opportunity, unfortunately, was more school. The University of Rome offered veterans the opportunity to get their bachelor's degree in two years instead of the regular five.

"What classes do you have in drawing?" Pietro had asked the registrar.

"This is a university, not an art school," the registrar responded.

Fortunately for Pietro, the enterprising assistant to the

registrar stepped in. "But I do see students in the engineering department drawing a lot."

"Engineering it is, then," Pietro decided before realizing that studying engineering might make him attractive to someone like his sister. Even thinking about that gives him an anxiety blister.

But studying engineering at university makes Pietro a lot less anxious than any of his high school subjects did. That's because he needs to focus only on what he's interested in. No more math. No more science. Actually, engineering encompasses both subjects, but when Pietro encounters a problem in engineering, the solution seems less abstract, more clear.

He takes classes at San Pietro in Vincoli, a historic church in Rome, and that's saying something in Rome. Popes and eminent artists lived at San Pietro in Vincoli. There was Pope Julius II, the warrior pope, and Luca Pacioli, the friar, mathematician, and father of accounting, the man who codified the double-entry bookkeeping method. Pietro is glad he doesn't have to study bookkeeping. Too many numbers. Too much math. And no drawing whatsoever. Pietro takes engineering classes in the converted convent where these men lived, worked, and studied. Leon Battista Alberti mentored Pacioli in these very rooms. Alberti didn't study bookkeeping, but he was a Renaissance man if there ever was one, shepherding architectural projects for the papacy, and even wetting his brush a few times as a painter.

Filippo Brunelleschi, the inventor of linear algebra, mentored Alberti. Alberti took Brunelleschi's findings and applied them to painting, writing the first treatise on how to apply mathematical perspective with a brush instead of a formula. Alberti passed his ideas down to the painter Piero della Francesca, then to Luca Pacioli. Pacioli couldn't paint, but he did comprehend these concepts and communicated them to painters, passing on the knowledge to Leonardo da Vinci, helping him parse the perspective in his *Last Supper*.

This cascade of ideas that all started with Brunelleschi now flows into Pietro, flooding him with inspiration, encouraging him to swim. Like these men, Pietro could be a Renaissance man, even though the Renaissance is long since over.

Not only did Brunelleschi invent linear algebra, but he also designed the dome of Il Duomo in Florence. Pietro has seen pictures, and he's seen detailed drawings that look a lot like pictures too. How could one man accomplish so much? Pietro hopes to find out, and that his drawing of Brunelleschi's dome will look as intricate as the ones he's seen in photos.

Pietro rides the train to Florence to study Brunelleschi's dome. Rimbaud got his start after the poet Paul Verlaine sent Rimbaud a train ticket to visit him in Paris. But Pietro doesn't need anyone to send him a ticket. His father still works for the railway and Pietro can get a ticket whenever he likes. It's one of the few benefits of having a father who works for the railway, but it's the only one Pietro needs right now. Although it doesn't matter if his father was a doctor or a proctor, a sailor or a tailor, as long as Pietro can get a train ticket whenever he wants. As you know, Pietro's never been too keen on classes, so when his teacher started talking about Il Duomo, Pietro decided he had to see it for himself.

As the train skims the countryside, Pietro reads:

In winter we'll travel in a little pink carriage
With cushions of blue.
We'll be fine. A nest of mad kisses waits
In each corner too.
You'll shut your eyes, not to see, through the glass,
Grimacing shadows of evening,
Those snarling monsters, a crowd going past
Of black wolves and black demons.
Then you'll feel your cheek tickled quite hard . . .
A little kiss, like a maddened spider,
Will run over your neck . . .
And you'll say: "Catch it!" bowing your head,
—And we'll take our time finding that creature
—Who travels so far . . .

Pietro's eyes wander out the train's window. It's not winter. And he has no love beside him, besides his love for Rimbaud. Pietro reads his poetry on the train. "That creature . . . who travels so far . . ." Pietro is one such creature, traveling by train to catch sight of a cathedral. Not like it's going anywhere. Construction on Il Duomo started in 1296, over six hundred years ago, and it's still standing, the largest masonry dome in the world. Oddly enough, the builders completed the cathedral in 1436, a hundred and forty years after they broke ground. And even though it took all that time, it was still groundbreaking when it was completed. When they began building the church, they didn't even know how to construct the dome. But they had faith it could be done. If not now, then by someone in the future. If not by them, then by someone in the next generation who could take their ideas and build what they envisioned. They were over a hundred years into the project before they had a competition to complete the project. Brunelleschi won, despite having no formal training in architecture.

Brunelleschi's design was audacious. It was brave. But when Brunelleschi died a decade after the dome's completion, he left no sketches, no drawings. How did he do it? Pietro's task for his engineering class is to figure out how Brunelleschi engineered its construction. How was it built with no central support structure? How did he get everything so high into the air? Did he use an ox-driven hoist? Would the herringbone-pattern bricks really support themselves during construction? How could you be sure?

As Pietro's classmates pore over drawings of the dome, Pietro climbs its stairs. Instead of studying drawings, he studies its rings. The dome is like a tree. And if Pietro looks closely enough, maybe he can decipher its history.

Pietro lies down on the floor of the Florence Cathedral. That's the name of the church, after all. Everyone calls it Il Duomo, though, because of the impressive dome.

Pietro would love to do something impressive after graduation. He wants to follow in Brunelleschi's footsteps. But there's no competition to enter and no fast track to success, to immortality. So, Pietro becomes a lowly housing inspector. While there's nothing lowly about being a housing inspector, especially in Rome, Pietro's antipathy toward the profession makes it such. All he can hope is that the job will give him a solid foundation from which to build. And as a housing inspector, his job is to make sure everything has a solid foundation. Who knows what's around the corner? Or in the ground? Especially as an inspector, you never know what you're going to unearth, what's waiting to swallow up your ambitions. Pietro knows that all too well. Being a housing inspector isn't quite what Pietro imagined he'd be doing with his life.

Pietro thought he'd travel, live life. And that's what brings him back to Rimbaud.

Pietro swims from shelf to shelf, using the bookstore as a lifeboat to keep his hopes afloat. He's been to Rimbaud's bookshelf repeatedly. But you know how bookstores are. Sometimes a book will float away from its shelf, and then someone needs to rescue it. Pietro doesn't mind being that person. He doesn't mind reshelving the books that have lost their way, even though he doesn't work in the shop.

Rimbaud saved Pietro on his own stormy sea. He helped him realize what life could be. That boy has been his buoy.

Pietro scans the nooks and crannies, dives into the shadows, the shallows, anywhere a rambling Rimbaud might be stowed. But today, there are no Rimbauds that need saving. There might be one soul who needs his services, though. A regal woman wades around Rimbaud's shelf, her fingertips tapping his tomes, her eyes roaming around the bookstore. Pietro swims over to her.

"Do you know anything about Rimbaud?" she inquires.

But Pietro doesn't answer her question directly. He recites: "'Once, if I recall correctly, my wife was a banquet.'"

Instead of being confused by his ruse, the woman joins in, "'The wine flowed. All hearts were open.'"

Pietro perks up. It's the same poem the ambulance driver used to perk him up when he needed saving. Evidently, this woman knows it as well as Pietro.

"So, you know Rimbaud, then," she summarizes, then switches gears. "What's your background?"

Pietro's eyebrows squish together. This woman is quite odd, isn't she? Who does she think she is, a queen? Pietro is at a loss for words, but she isn't.

"What do you do? Did you fight in the war?" she continues.

"I did. And now I'm a . . ." Pietro fumbles, partly because he isn't proud of his current occupation, and partly because he wants to know why she's peppering him with all these questions. "Why do you want to know? What's this all about, anyway?"

Now it's the woman's turn to perk up. She sets herself. Shoulders back. Face slack. But her eyes are sharp, like she's about to attack.

"I'm Countess Irene di Robilant," she announces. "I've been tasked with locating a veteran to award an exchange fellowship. It's for a year of study in the United States." Her eyes cast downward. "The process has been a bit tiring, to be honest, trying to find someone who meets the right qualifications. So, I decided I'd award the fellowship to the first fine fellow to approach this shelf and have a passing knowledge of Rimbaud. Anyone who loves Rimbaud's vivid accounts of foreign travel must be up for such an exchange, don't you think?"

Pietro stares back at her. He can't believe what she's saying. She's either a lunatic or one of the most luminous women he's ever met.

The countess cocks her head. "So, what do you think? Are you the man I've been looking for, ready to sail to a distant shore?"

Pietro's lips press together. His chest suddenly wants to be an anchor. Sail to America? Just pack up and leave? And he'd have to study? More school? What would he even study? How would he figure that out? How would he figure any of this out?

Then Pietro chuckles. The men who built Il Duomo began the church before they even had a way to construct its eponymous dome. Perhaps it's Pietro's turn to be as audacious, as brave. He'll figure out how to do it when the time is right.

So, is he ready to sail to America? Is he ready to sail to a distant shore?

"Yes," Pietro says.

Let's see what this adventure has in store.

Chapter Eight

ELEVEN SUITS

What to pack?

The journey will last eleven days. Or at least that's how long the voyage across the ocean will take. Then how long to Cornell once he's in New York? What do they wear in Cornell? Or rather, *at* Cornell. The university is in Ithaca, New York, but it's named after its founder. How did Mr. Cornell dress? Do the people there still dress like him?

Pietro has never quite had a passion for fashion. In fact, one could look at his sense of style with a bit of compassion. Often, his socks don't even match. Who cares if your socks match? Hardly anyone ever sees them, especially with how tight the cuffs on most pants are. The fabric of Pietro's trousers nearly touches his socks. Someone would see them only if he sat down. And Pietro doesn't enjoy sitting down for too long.

Perhaps a tailor would know how Pietro should pack. He wanders into the tailor's shop to find a row of men waiting for him. All are bespeckled in their bespoke suits, small spots of color cropping up here and there, on a collar, a pocket square, or a pair of socks. Some of these men are standing, but Pietro can already see specks of color poking out, their shoes not quite touching the cuffs of their pants. Men on the street don't look like this, not yet, so what type of fashion are these men selling?

Pietro approaches the man who looks the busiest. Or at least the one with the busiest suit. His cravat is so intricate, you could mistake it for a lady's hat. There are two sets of buttons on the front of his suit, which is a feminine shade of pink. His shoulders are wider than most men's, though. Or maybe they're wider than his waist. He's not so much flamboyant as he is flamingly buoyant, his outfit elevating himself above his peers like cream rising to the top, searing himself into Pietro's corneas. That's one way to be memorable. Despite the color, the cut of his suit makes him look more masculine than the others.

"I'm traveling to New York. What should I pack?" Pietro asks before he introduces himself. "I'm Pietro, by the way."

The man inhales, winds up. "I will not sell you clothes, *signore*. I will introduce you to a new way of life. And you can refer to me as Gianni."

Pietro wiggles his eyebrows in amusement. Gianni raises his. Is Pietro trying to wink at him?

"How are you traveling to America?" Gianni asks.

"I'm sailing on the *Conte Rosso*."

"Ooh, fancy boy. I attended a soiree on that ship. She's a new one, isn't she? And all decked out for a party. Excuse the pun. Unless you're up for a bit of fun." Gianni winks at Pietro. "She's a palace on the ocean. Paneled ceilings. Red carpets on the stairs. Crystal chandeliers. Don't grab on to those if the ship starts sinking. But I'm sure I don't have to tell you that."

Pietro swallows, not knowing how to respond. He continues with business as usual, even though this is anything but. "How many suits do you think I need?"

Gianni looks Pietro up and down, taking in his figure, but also trying to figure out what type of man he is. "How many days does the crossing take?"

"Eleven."

"Well, then you'll need eleven suits, won't you?"

"Eleven? Isn't that excessive?"

Gianni scoffs. "Sailing on the *Conte Rosso* is all about being excessive. You're not going for *sprezzatura*, are you? You don't want to blend into the background. You're going to America, so dress American. Stand out."

That word. "*Sprezza—*" Pietro hasn't heard it before.

"Oh, good," Gianni jumps in. "It's better that you're not a disciple of *sprezzatura*. You don't want any of this 'effortless elegance.' Americans want you to see how much effort they've put into their clothing. That's why they wear wool suits, along with the English, isn't it? Wool absorbs a third of its own weight in water and still appears dry. It's like they want to show you how much sweat they've put into their garment. There's no avoiding affectation. Affectation is a celebration!" Gianni throws his hands into the air.

Pietro puts his in his pockets. "I guess I want to stand out."

"Good. Now, let's see what we have." Gianni whirls around

the shop, snatching suits off the racks. "Right after the war, all the men's suits looked like military uniforms. Jackets cut very trim and long, with the buttons going nearly up to the neck. Ghastly, if you ask me. I mean, it's always becoming to see a man in uniform, but a suit is not a uniform, you know what I mean?"

Gianni places suits into a pile. There's one with pinstripes. A light gray one. Then a purple one. Green. Another with pinstripes, but this one in aquamarine. "So many men wear these hourglass suits now, even some of my associates." Gianni gestures over to them. "It makes their shoulders the same width as their hips, then they cinch it in at the waist, giving them an hourglass figure. But they're not women. So why do they dress as one? Men should be men, don't you think?"

"Yes . . . I guess so," Pietro says.

"All these suits I'm giving you," Gianni continues, gesturing to himself, "broad shoulders, more fabric in the chest, no cinch, and they taper down to your waist, creating a triangle. Do you see it? Triangles are strong. The strongest shape, they say. Much more masculine. It'll be all the rage soon enough. And you'll be at the forefront of that fashion. Lucky you. And the pants. No more tight cuffs at the bottom. No, we'll make them a foot wide. Eleven and a half inches, to be precise. You'll have big legs. More room for your manliness, if you know what I mean. You'll take up more space, and people love doing that in America."

Gianni snags two tuxedos from the rack. "One in white and one in black, because you don't want to be caught with the wrong color for the occasion, now, do you?"

Pietro nods. He didn't know what to pack, but with all these suits, and their price, he might have a heart attack. "How much will all this cost? I don't know if I can afford it."

"It will be a small price to pay for what they afford you," Gianni promises.

Pietro shuffles out of the store, all eleven suits in tow. Nine suits and two tuxedos, actually. Pietro can't believe he bought them all. Where did he get the gall?

But all his anxiety goes out the porthole when he boards the ship in one of his shiny new suits. All eyes are on him, and he finds he's the belle of the ball. No, he's the triangle of the ball, looking quite different from the squares in their hourglass-shaped suits.

Pietro promenades around the promenade. He lounges in the lounge's leather chairs. This ship is a palace on the ocean and Pietro is its prince. The *Conte Rosso* was built a decade after the Titanic sank, and it was the first transatlantic liner built after the war and the largest Italian liner to date. But even if this ship were to start sinking, Pietro's confidence could keep it afloat.

He has a new suit for every day of the journey, which quickly makes him the talk of the ship.

"Has he repeated any of his suits?"

"What will he wear tomorrow?"

Pietro hears people whisper as he passes them on the promenade.

"I see you haven't read Baldassare Castiglione's *The Book of the Courtier*," an older gentleman in an equally ostentatious suit says to Pietro.

Pietro rubs his neck, not knowing what the man is talking about. It was all smooth sailing, but now he's hit an iceberg.

"Don't worry," the man assuages him. "Neither have I." He plucks a pink cravat out of his pocket. "I usually transform my ensemble once we pass the halfway point of the passage, but you've inspired me to throw caution to the wind."

"I'm Pietro Belluschi, sir," he says, jutting his hand out in front of him, eager to make friends with the gentleman.

The man takes it. "My name is Don Gelasio Caetani. What brings you to America?"

"I have a fellowship to study at Cornell for a year."

"Why, that's marvelous. You know, I had a fellowship to study at Columbia, focused on engineering. How about you?"

"I studied engineering in Rome," Pietro says.

"Well, that's two things we have in common now." Caetani smiles.

"So, you're an engineer?"

"Unfortunately, I'm something less useful these days," Caetani says coyly. "I'm the Italian ambassador to the United States."

A flush sweeps across Pietro's cheeks.

"And it would be my delight," Caetani continues, "if you would join me for dinner." Caetani notices Pietro's reddening face. "Don't turn into a lobster, son. I think that's what they're serving."

Pietro laughs, the first of many. Pietro and Caetani get along swimmingly. So much so that the ambassador insists Pietro eat with him every night. He wants a front-row seat to what Pietro's going to wear next. Unlike most ships, the *Conte Rosso* has an outdoor dining area. But the indoor dining room is larger, and at night the lights are brighter inside. Caetani makes sure they get a table in the center of the room so everyone can take in Pietro's fashion show.

"After we get to America," Caetani says on the last night of the crossing, "I don't want this show to end. So, please, reach out if you ever need any help."

Pietro smiles. In one sentence, the suits have paid for themselves.

Chapter Nine

SPEAK EASY

She's green, but she's not seasick. If only Pietro weren't. While the ocean voyage has been pleasant, it hasn't been the most accommodating to his insides. Outwardly, Pietro has been a paragon of civility, donning his stylish suits. But inside, his stomach has gone for quite the ride. He could have sworn his face turned as green as Lady Liberty's during the voyage, and now, gazing upon her as she greets him to her golden shore, his face is white. But he's not fearful. The blood in his face has merely migrated to his chest, along with the rest of the blood in his body. Pietro's heart pounds. *Thump. Thump.* It's quite an interesting sound.

Pietro's mouth opens, inhaling the sea air. He gulps it down as if it were his last breath before diving into the icy depths. He's about to experience an unknown world. America is not so new, approaching almost a hundred and fifty years as a nation, but compared to Italy, almost anything seems new. That's why Pietro was so curious to see this new colossus. Pietro had heard about her, this woman who sought to unseat the Colossus of Rhodes, that Old Wonder of the World. And she did. The Colossus of Rhodes was 108 feet tall, whereas this new beauty is 151 feet on her own, and 305 including her base.

Instead of celebrating the sun, this wondrous woman celebrates her sons and her daughters, and anyone else "yearning to breathe free," as the poet Emma Lazarus immortalized on a plaque at her feet.

Pietro has heard about the plaque. He's heard about this Colossus. But no one could have explained this emotion as he gazes upon the green goddess. He is utterly without words, but he isn't so tight-lipped when he visits Grand Central Terminal. They say Grand Central Terminal is one of the grandest sights of the city, but all Pietro can see is an eyesore.

Green. No, not quite. Maybe aquamarine. Pietro had heard Grand Central's ceiling was cerulean blue, like the color of a calm sky, but this color has more in common with the green patina of Lady Liberty than it does with the sky or serenity, especially because it's leaking. Pietro stares up at the patches of white, black, and green mildew spewing across the ceiling like little comets. The water damage blends into the other celestial designs, but only because the rest of the ceiling is backwards. East is west. West is east. If a sailor used this ceiling to navigate to the new world, he'd never find it.

Perhaps they'll get it right one day. Grand Central is only five decades old, but it is already on its third iteration. First it was the Grand Central Depot, then it was rebuilt as Grand Central Station, and now it's Grand Central Terminal. Pietro hopes this iteration lives up to its name and ends there. He imagines it won't be too long until someone tears it down and starts over again with a new name and a new design. Pietro traveled all the way to the new world, but he finds the old one staring back at him in the Grand Central Terminal's Beaux-Arts design.

Pietro spots a student sitting on the steps, sketching the high arched windows that allow the sunlight to dapple onto the concourse.

"What are you doing? Why are you copying this?" Pietro asks him incredulously. Perhaps Pietro could have been less incredulous himself, especially because he too was once tasked with drawing existing buildings back in Rome when he was a student. But they aren't in Rome; they're in New York City. It is a new world full of new possibilities. So, he asks, "Why are you still clinging to the past?"

"Excuse me?" the student responds. "What did you say?"

Pietro's face goes flush. He spoke to the student in Italian, not English, so perhaps these Americans aren't the only ones to blame for lingering in the past. Pietro needs to communicate with this student in his own lingo. Pietro's only problem is that he doesn't know much English.

"What . . . ?" Pietro struggles to ask, searching for the right words but feeling as completely turned around as the ceiling. Finally, Pietro points at the student's sketch and hunches his shoulders.

The student nods. "Oh, it's an assignment for school."

Pietro scans the station. His attention was on the ceiling,

but he now sees nearly a hundred students, all tucked into the nooks and crannies of the station, sketching its various nooks and crannies.

He turns to the student. *Are these your fellow students? Where do you study?* These are the questions Pietro would like to ask, but he doesn't know how.

"Where . . ." Pietro's face contorts, trying to come up with the semblance of a question.

"Here," the student says.

Pietro's eyes go wide. "How . . ." *Can you study in a train station?*

Luckily, the student understands Pietro's consternation. "On the sixth floor, at the new art school."

Pietro nods, then climbs the stairs to the sixth floor. He has to see this art school for himself. New students in a new building studying old designs. Is this what his education in America will be like? But when he gets to the sixth floor, Pietro doesn't see a school, but rather a gigantic art gallery.

"Welcome to the largest art gallery in the world," an attendant says.

Pietro nods but doesn't respond. How could he? Pietro wanders around the gallery. He thought he heard the man say it was the largest gallery in the world, but it's nowhere near as large as the Uffizi in Florence. As he meanders around the gallery, Pietro sees something odd. Next to every painting, every statue . . . why does everything seem to be on sale?

Against one wall, one painting stands out amongst them all. An old man hunches over next to a fallen tree, sketching its fallen corpse. Pietro can't think of a more fitting metaphor for what he's seen in this building, people immortalizing dead things instead of creating something new. He goes to the small plaque next to the painting and copies the words: "*The Artist Sketching* by John Singer Sargent." He's heard of the painter, but he must look up what the title means.

Perhaps his hotel will have a dictionary. He hasn't checked in yet. The sight of the Statue of Liberty gave him enough energy to lug his luggage uptown to see Grand Central Terminal, but now he's quite tired. Pietro needs to lie down. It's too bad his hotel is back downtown.

Although Pietro is in a new city, he can see his hometown all around him. He walks past the New York City Public Library. He can tell the Pantheon in Rome inspired its facade. Pietro knows a thing or two about architecture. Or at least that's what he's going to study at Cornell. But with all the buildings inspired by architecture back home, perhaps he'll be the one to teach them a few things.

Pietro lumbers over to his hotel, ready for slumber. He sets his bags down and stumbles backward for a second before he regains his composure.

"Had too much to drink already?" the man at the door asks. "Don't know if I'll be able to let you in until you sober up."

But Pietro can't understand a word he's saying. Pietro pulls out a piece of paper with the hotel's address on it, the hotel the countess had arranged for him, and shows it to the man.

"You're in the right place," he says, eyeing Pietro up and down. "Suppose it's better for you to be drunk inside rather than out in the street." He opens the door for Pietro, who gathers his things and heads inside.

But this is no hotel. There is one man sleeping, but that's on the bar, and only for a second until the bartender slams down a beer and the man jolts awake, as if the liquid were giving him life.

"So, what'll you have?" the bartender asks Pietro.

Pietro looks around. It's clear he's not in the right place, but how can he communicate where he should be and then understand how to get there?

He sets down his bags and pulls his hands up to his face, using his hands to mime pillows.

"Yeah, you looking for the hotel?" the bartender asks. "That's upstairs." He points upward.

Pietro looks up at the ceiling. It has more stains than Grand Central Terminal. He grimaces, then looks back at the bartender.

"No," the bartender says, shaking his head. "You need to go upstairs." He uses his fingers to mime climbing stairs.

Pietro nods and smiles for a second before his tiredness tugs his lips back into a frown. Pietro exhales. That wasn't as difficult as he thought it would be, but it still took a toll.

Pietro climbs the stairs, checks in, finds his bed, and rests his head. If only he could go to sleep. Everything in his body tells him it's time for some shut-eye. If only he could shut his ears. A cacophony emanates from the speakeasy below. A discordant mix of yelling clashes with glass bottles smashing against the ground. Must be time for another round. Feet shuffle. There's a scuffle. No . . . a fight. Pietro puts his head in his hands. It's going to be a long night.

Pietro thought alcohol was outlawed in America, but apparently the patrons at this establishment aren't as well-versed in the law as he is. Pietro tries to shut out the noise, but it builds and builds, almost as if it were climbing stairs, almost as if it were busting down his door. Then, all of a sudden, Pietro finds himself on the floor.

He looks around his room. He's surrounded by police, who've upended his bed and discovered a stash of liquor beneath it.

There wasn't a brawl. No, that wasn't it at all. It was a raid.

"Is this your liquor, boy?" a gruff police officer asks.

Pietro freezes, partly out of nerves and partly out of exasperation.

"No, it's not his, Tully," the bartender answers behind him. "It's that sacramental wine I was storing for you, don't you remember?" he says with a wink.

"Oh, I forgot all about that." The police officer smiles. "Grab a bottle, boys. Help me . . . confiscate this stuff."

All the officers grab a bottle or two, or a crate. They laugh as they exit. Tonight will be a long night. For them, it's going to be great.

But what's going on? Pietro couldn't tell you. He only knows that before the last officer leaves, the one who spoke to him plops a bottle in his hands.

"This one is yours," he says before exiting with the bartender.

Although he can't read the label, Pietro knows it's liquor. And he knows he's not supposed to drink it, especially because he's a foreigner in the United States during Prohibition and he doesn't want to do anything that would send him home. But people don't always do what they're supposed to. The speakeasy didn't. Neither did the police. So, why should he?

Pietro grips the bottle and joins the party downstairs, which is already as loud as it was during the raid. There is no way he is going to sleep through this, so he may as well join in on the fun. Who knows, maybe downing the bottle will help him shut out the noise or at least help him speak a little easier.

Chapter Ten

THE COLD OF WINTER

Gray sky. Gray suit. "Go Big Red!"

Pietro looks out the window as his fellow students stream out of his dorm screaming for their team.

"Do you want to come with us?" his neighbor asks behind him.

Pietro looks at the young man, then at the packs of people parading over to the stadium. He can't quite understand what the gentleman asked, but he can put two and two together. You need not speak a language to understand context.

"*Un momento*," Pietro says in Italian before switching to English. "One moment."

He ducks into his closet. Red . . . red . . . He has almost a dozen suits and none of them are red? Pietro grabs the purple one. It's the closest he has to the red everyone else is wearing. That carnelian red, as it is officially known, or more fittingly, Cornellian Red. Pietro wants to fit in. He wants to be just like any of the other students, but he sticks out like a sore thumb as he stands in the stadium in his suit.

Everyone else wears sweaters and caps emblazoned with big Cs on them, their regalia on full display as they regale each other with tales of previous games.

"Columbia didn't see it coming! Fifty-six to zero," his neighbor says.

"And our second string scored half those points!" a young man next to him joins in.

"Three hundred and thirty-nine to twenty-seven. That's how much we dominated last year. On average, we scored more points per game than everyone else did against us the whole season."

"The only game that wasn't a blowout was Penn."

Pietro listens intently as the two men chat, his ears open for keywords he might use to decipher their conversation. Pietro shrugs. Or is it a shiver? Pietro's suit is double-breasted, which provides some additional warmth, but he can't believe he forgot to pack a coat. The wind sweeps across his chest and finds its way past his lapels, searing his insides. Pietro will always remember this cold, this numbing chill that pierces him to his bones.

Everyone on the Cornell side of the crowd chants, "Go Big Red! Go Big Red!" Pietro joins in, parroting them and any other words they scream.

"Give 'em hell, Cornell!" Pietro hollers after he hears another man yell it.

His neighbor laughs. Pietro scrutinizes his face. Is he laughing at Pietro?

"You're going to fit right in," his neighbor says before slapping Pietro on the back.

Pietro smiles. His body shakes, but this time it's not from the cold. He wants to fit in so badly he can't stand still. He wants to find a place for himself here. And the next day, Cornell gives him an opportunity to find one in the form of a placement exam. Pietro is a graduate student, but the school wants to make sure he's qualified to take graduate-level courses. Or, as his advisors explain, they want to determine "which classes might be the best fit."

Pietro stares at the exam. It may as well be in Greek. Actually, growing up in Ancona, he's learned a bit of Greek, so he might do better if it were in that language.

Pietro panics. He flips through the pages. He can't understand any of this . . . until he sees a math problem. Mathematics is a beautiful language, isn't it? That's what Pietro concludes as he scans the second half of the test. It doesn't matter what language you speak as long as you understand numbers. Pietro can decipher these questions, but everything else on the test is a mystery to him.

Pietro fidgets as he sits in his desk, waiting for the exam proctor to tabulate his results. Even though he knows he did poorly on at least half of the exam, he still holds a modicum of hope that he passed. But all hope fades away as the proctor ambles up to him and says, "I'm sorry, son. You did well enough on the second section, but it looks like you should stick to undergraduate courses."

Even though Pietro doesn't understand every word of that sentence, he reads the man's face and knows he failed.

~

I'm a failure.

Pietro ruminates in his room. He looks out at the gray sky. The sun peeks through the clouds but fails to break through. Pietro is like the sun. All he needs to do is break through these clouds. He didn't come to the United States to fail. He can't go home until he's a success. And to do that, he needs to learn English.

So, Pietro studies English the same way he trained for war. He wakes up at four in the morning. Every day. Mornings are cold at Cornell. So, he wraps himself in blankets, using them as armor as he drills himself on vocabulary, grammar, and syntax. Then he uses breakfast as his first exercise of the day, using everyone else's grogginess to his own tactical advantage, steering conversations to areas he's more comfortable with. He converts football games and dining halls to training grounds, building his conversation skills.

As he becomes more and more comfortable with the language, he becomes more and more frustrated with the type of work he's doing in his architecture courses. In one class, he's tasked with designing a new library. Pietro takes the task seriously. Instead of scrounging through his architectural design history books, though, he uses the assignment as an opportunity to interrogate his fellow students:

"How do you use the library?"

"How long do you stay here? And why do you leave?"

"Do you prefer natural or artificial light when you're studying?"

Pietro hasn't realized he's become quite comfortable with the language until he shows a preliminary sketch of his design to his professor, who asks, "Hm. Have you thought about adding three arches out front, like the New York Public Library?"

Pietro scrunches his face. "Why would I add something like that to this library? What function does it provide? You asked me to design a *new* library, not produce a copy of a copy of a copy of one. I want to study architecture, not history."

Unfortunately, Pietro's professor doesn't recognize the ease in which Pietro speaks, but concentrates on his insubordination instead. "Well . . . I never . . ." the professor says, having his own struggle with the language before turning on his heel and walking away.

Needless to say, Pietro failed the assignment. But he succeeded in something much more important. He expressed himself in English, confidently. And now he can see the man he wants to be.

Even though Pietro long ago bought himself a coat, the winter cold at Cornell always found a way to creep into his bones. But now he senses an intensity brewing inside, emanating outward like the sun.

As his year at Cornell draws to a close, Pietro senses the light inside him. It burns, but it still can't penetrate the clouds. While he's mastered the English language, he hasn't become a success.

So, Pietro writes a letter to his shipmate and friend

Ambassador Caetani, espousing his desire to stay in America to pursue his idea of the American dream, conquer the continent, and manifest his destiny.

"I've accomplished so much this past year, but can't imagine returning to Italy until I've achieved the success I know I am capable of," Pietro writes him. "I know you can recognize that burning desire, that fiery passion that burns inside you to prove yourself worthy and make Italy proud."

Pietro grins at the letter he's written. He's so assured in his newfound literary ability that he doesn't even ask anyone to double-check the document before sending it off to Caetani in New York City.

Luckily, Pietro doesn't have to wait long for his reply. Caetani offers to set him up with a job as a mining engineer in Kellogg, Idaho, where Caetani once worked himself.

It's not quite the leg up Pietro was expecting, but with no other options, he crosses the continent to Idaho. Unfortunately, he finds the cold of winter made the journey with him. No matter what he does, he can't find a coat to keep out the cold. Pietro can never get warm—until summer arrives, and then he can never cool down.

In Idaho, water flows in the streams. If only Pietro could drink from them. The mining operation contaminates the water, making it undrinkable. And then the streams freeze over again in the winter and the cycle continues.

As the days become shorter, leading into another long winter, the light inside Pietro dims. America isn't quite what he expected. And his job isn't quite what he expected either. He thought he would be a mining engineer, but his job mostly entails standing around in the cold, handing tools to an electrician. A trained monkey could do this work, but then again, so could a tool belt. Mozart might have been a trained monkey, but at least he was the one performing.

Pietro learns a bit of mining lingo and a bit about mining itself, but more than anything, he realizes he needs to figure out how to dig himself out of this pit.

"I think I've gone bust," Pietro tells his boss.

"What do you mean? We've been hitting all our quotas. Lead. Silver. Even been getting a bit of gold out of the shaft."

"No, it's a metaphor," Pietro explains. "I think I've gone bust. Here. I don't think I can do this job much longer."

"Well, I'd be lying if I said it didn't disappoint me to hear you say that. You came so well recommended from Mr. Caetani," his boss explains. "Thought I'd struck gold. But I guess that's the whole point, isn't it?"

Pietro tilts his head to the side. "What do you mean?"

"Like you said, you've gone bust here. You don't want to help find someone else's gold. You want to find your own."

"Yeah, I guess that's about right," Pietro agrees.

"Well," his boss exhales, "I think I know a vein you could explore."

Chapter Eleven

THE PORTLAND TRAIL

"Why should I hire you?" asks A. E. Doyle, a spectacled man with hair neatly combed over to the side, as his eyes scan a letter.

Pietro shifts in his chair. "Because I came all the way here. To you. To Portland. Heard you were the busiest architect on the West Coast. Had the most work coming in and out of your office. So, I thought you'd need the most help."

Doyle looks up from the letter. "So, I should hire you because you know how to buy a train ticket?"

"No, I—"

"You only just sent me this letter. Got it in the mail today. So, why couldn't you wait for my reply?"

"I thought my letter might not fully explain my eagerness, or my potential, sir."

"*Sir*? Don't call me *sir*. I hate it when people call me that. Or *boss*. Don't call me *boss* either. Makes my skin crawl. Call me Eddie, like everyone else. I am the boss, though, so don't forget that."

Eddie's eyes go back to the letter, and he sits back in his chair.

Pietro leans forward, eager to keep the conversation going. But what can he say? Perhaps something obvious and innocuous? "Is Eddie short for Edward?" he says.

"No," Eddie exhales. "Who told you that?"

"No, I—no one, I—"

"Middle name is Ernest, if you must know."

"Then why do you go by Eddie?"

Eddie sets down the letter. "I once knew a guy named Nick. Want to know why they called him that? Was it short for Nicholas? No. As a kid, he used to get into a lot of scraps. Always had something on his face, some nick or scratch. So they called him Nick, even though his real name was Donald. You see?"

Pietro nods, trying to make it seem like he understands. "I see, but how does that—"

"Is this interview about me or is it about you?"

"Sorry, s—" Pietro almost says *sir* but changes it to, "Sorry, sorry, Eddie."

"Can you draw?"

"Yes."

"And you're Italian."

"Yes."

"That wasn't a question. I can tell from your accent. Lucky for you, I'm about to sail over to Italy, relax a bit, maybe see some architecture. Doctors tell me I have to take it easy. And because I have to take it easy I may as well get some work done. What buildings should I check out when I'm there? What do you like?"

Pietro's mouth opens. He hadn't expected this question. "I, uh—there's *Il Duomo.*"

"No! New buildings! I've already seen that. I want to see what's new."

"I, uh, saw some drawings by Antonio Sant'Elia."

"But not a finished building?"

"No, I—they haven't afforded him the opportunity yet."

"Well, I must seek him out when I'm there."

Pietro's mouth opens but no sound comes out. He remembers Antonio Sant'Elia died in the Great War, but he can't correct his error now. All he can utter is, "Yes, you should."

But Eddie doesn't seem all that concerned with Pietro's deception, or anything having to do with Pietro, actually. And that's because he's in pain. Eddie doubles over, hugs his waist tightly, and breathes in and out with a quick huff.

Pietro stands up. "Are you all right?"

"Yes, I'm—it'll pass. Just you wait. Doctors say this should subside soon enough." Eddie rocks back and forth, trying to get back to the business at hand. "Remind me, do you draw?"

"Yes," Pietro answers warily.

"Good. Then you know how to trace," Eddie responds between breaths. "You're going to trace all the drawings we give you. And you're going to do that until you prove you can do something else. I'll start you at twenty dollars."

Pietro smiles, his insides screaming: *I got the job!* But then he cocks his head. "Is that twenty dollars a week or twenty dollars a month?"

Eddie scrunches his face, but it's clear it's not from the pain. "What do you think?"

Pietro doesn't know what to think, except that it would be wise for him not to ask another follow-up question. Luckily, he doesn't have to.

"Report to Charles Greene in the design department. He'll get you started."

Pietro hops to his feet and bobs up and down on his way out. "Thank you, s—thank you, Eddie."

Pietro exits the office, scanning the work floor on his way out. Dozens of men hunch around crowded work tables, all wearing white smocks to keep the charcoal and other creative debris off their clothes.

On a wall across the work floor, opposite Eddie's office, Pietro spots blues, pinks, and reds radiating outward in a spiral, almost as if they were trying to hypnotize him. That must be the design department. Soaring above the space is a model mock-up of a roofline unlike one he's ever seen before. It's almost like an A-frame, but the sides have a slight slope to them. And it has triangle-shaped cutouts, or some sort of design, near the top. Whatever they are, Pietro wants to find out.

He marches up to a man underneath the mock-up, the only man not wearing a smock on the entire work floor, the only man not actively working on something. Instead, he's reading.

"Is this the design department?" Pietro asks, but the man

doesn't look up from his book. Pietro scratches his neck while he waits. He rocks back and forth for a second before trying to introduce himself again. "I'm here to report to Charles Greene in the design department."

"I am not *in* the design department. I am the *head* of the design department," the man says, still not looking up from his book. "And you may call me Mr. Greene."

"Yes, of course," Pietro says. Then he waits for his first set of instructions.

But Mr. Greene doesn't give any. He just continues reading his book.

Pietro's eyes wander to the mock-up above. His mind wonders what could break the tension between them.

"Is this a new style of roofline?" Pietro asks.

Mr. Greene's eyes shoot above him, then ricochet back at Pietro. "So, your question is, is an *irimoya* roofline a new style of roofline?"

Pietro senses a sharp pain in his stomach. Did he just contract whatever is afflicting Eddie? Pietro's jacket squeezes his chest like a corset and all he's able to squeak out is, "Yes?"

Mr. Greene sighs. "No, it is not a new style. The irimoya roofline is an ancient form in Japanese architecture. So, now that you've asked me a question, let me ask you one." Mr. Greene sets down his book and leans forward. "What the hell do you think you know about architecture?"

Pietro inhales all the oxygen and courage he can muster. "I studied engineering at the University of Rome, and architecture for a year at Cornell."

"I asked what you know, not where you studied," Mr. Greene dismisses. "Must have been nice getting that fancy education. I had to learn almost everything I know from books like this." He picks up the book he was reading for emphasis. "And you still haven't learned what an irimoya roofline looks like."

Mr. Greene stands up and starts circling Pietro. "What's the difference between stucco and glazed terra-cotta?"

Pietro winces. "Well, you apply stucco by—"

"I know how you apply stucco, but do you really think I'm asking you how you apply it? We're an architecture firm, not a builder. What's the structural difference?"

Pietro looks up, but the irimoya roofline won't save him. "I don't know."

"Let's try another one. What's the difference between architecture in Italy and architecture in Portland?"

"I've only just arrived."

"And where were you before?"

"Idaho."

"Ah, so even less of an excuse. Because even if you just arrived in the West, you should have figured it out on the train. What was on either side of the train, for miles and miles?"

Pietro's eyes light up, but he's afraid to answer.

"It's not a riddle," Mr. Greene says, ostensibly to assure Pietro, but doing no such thing.

"Trees," Pietro posits.

"Yes, that's right. So, you probably won't be too surprised to hear the crucial difference between architecture in Italy and architecture here is that we use a lot of wood, whereas you're used to seeing a lot of masonry and stucco, aren't you?"

"Yes, I—"

"I've learned a lot about Italian architecture. Eddie even sent me there for research. Did you know Leonardo da Vinci designed buildings? He was brilliant, even though he didn't get a formal education either. And look at him now." Mr. Greene steps forward, gesturing around the work floor. "I started here as an office boy. I rose through the ranks, one rung at a time. So, please know that when I say I am the head of the design department . . . I am not only the head of the design department. I *am* the design department. And I will not wait for others to recognize my brilliance."

"Are you giving him your speech?" Eddie asks, swooping in.

Pietro's eyes search Eddie's, hoping he's not just swooping in but that he'll be Pietro's savior.

"Seems like your new boy is greener than I am," Mr. Greene says dryly.

Eddie laughs, then it turns into a quick cough, which he covers up. "I'm heading out, Charlie. Start him on a new stack when you're done giving your . . . orientation." But before he leaves, Eddie turns to Pietro. "Pay attention to Charlie and you might have his job one day."

Pietro looks at Eddie as he hobbles out of the office. Then he turns back to Mr. Greene, who's gone back to his book. Pietro inhales, swallows his nerves back down into this throat. "Is that why you're studying that Japanese roofline? Because they use a lot of wood in Japan as well?"

Mr. Greene shuts his book and gives Pietro a look. "That doesn't prove you know anything. It just proves you can listen."

"And I want to listen," Pietro assures him, "especially to someone as brilliant as yourself."

"Do you know how to draw?"

"I love drawing," Pietro says emphatically, before regaining his composure. "But I'm sure I could learn a lot from someone like you."

"Oh, I'm sure you could." Mr. Greene eyes Pietro up and down.

Pietro's muscles tighten. He hasn't had a man scan him up and down like that since the man who sold him the suits.

"But *why* do you love drawing?" Mr. Greene continues.

"I—I don't know, really," Pietro stammers. He furrows his brow, narrows his eyes. "It's just something I started doing, and then I couldn't get it out of my head. Couldn't get enough of it. Sort of like this rush that bubbles up inside me and shoots out my fingers onto the page."

The corners of Mr. Greene's lips curl up into a smile. He stands, shakes Pietro's hand. "Welcome to the design department."

Pietro beams, unclenches, until Mr. Greene speaks again.

"Your initiation begins tonight."

Chapter Twelve

FAREWELL

"Imagine you're sitting in a forest," a man's voice says. "Only thin strands of sunlight penetrate the canopy. Thin little specks of light dapple their way to the forest floor, stretching all the way down to your face, like tiny pinpricks. But they don't cause pain. It's delightful. It enlivens you; your skin takes that sunshine and infuses it into your soul."

Pietro opens his eyes. He loves this exercise. Although guided meditation lowers his heart rate, he's always invigorated afterward, as if he just went for a hike. Pietro loves going for hikes and drinking the cool, unpolluted water from the streams, something he couldn't do in Idaho. He loves wandering around the forest.

Wanderlust pumps through his veins. Pietro's wanderlust has more to do with the German origin of the word than the American use of it. *Wanderlust* made its voyage across the Atlantic a couple decades before Pietro. It originated from German, combining the words *wandern* (to hike) and *Lust* (desire). But like many things, transformation occurs when you take something from one place and put it in another. For Americans, the word means to travel, to expose yourself to unfamiliar cultures, to find yourself while getting lost, whereas Germans use it to express their love of hiking.

Pietro senses a transformation occurring within him too. He's shifting, becoming different, still possessing a core definition of himself but opening up to opportunities to redefine who he is. A large part of that has to do with his initiation into the design department. Pietro has a lot to be nervous about when Mr. Greene tells him about his upcoming initiation. Pietro had seen young men at Cornell undergo their own (often ludicrous) initiations into their (often lucrative) fraternities, and he wonders whether Mr. Greene has something like that in mind for him. Would he have to slaughter a chicken? Perhaps dress up like a barmaid and go around asking other men for a date? But Mr. Greene has nothing like that in mind. Rather, he brings Pietro to a basement—not initially a good sign—in an art museum, an odd choice of location to humiliate someone, where he initiates Pietro into a series of art classes.

The man leading the classes and this guided meditation is Harry Wentz. Pietro likes to think of him as less of a man and more of a mantra, though. "Sense the spring . . . Sense the spring . . ." It's a phrase you can repeat over and over as you meditate, the repetition of the words drowning out the noise in your brain. The calming words rush over you, flushing out your anxious energy. Your attention focuses on one thing so your mind can become unfocused. So you can tap into the well of creativity within you, that place deep inside where ideas come from.

Now, Pietro grew up in Italy. He became a man in Rome, surrounded by some of the greatest works of art in the world. But it's here, in a basement in Portland, where Pietro learns that a piece of art is not just an object; it's a process, something you learn and repeat over and over, similar to a mantra.

In this way, Pietro's initiation into the art classes has turned into a culmination. Everything leading up to now, all his experiences, pool together as part of his subconscious, something just outside his sight, part of a spring he can tap into, a creative well he can drink from. As the months pass, Pietro graduates from being a novitiate in the process to a full-fledged practitioner.

So, today, when Harry brings the class out of the guided meditation exercise, Pietro doesn't notice the art surrounding him. He's connected to the art inside himself. He's connecting to Harry's belief that you can apply the process of artistic creation to any form, any medium, whether it be painting, sculpture, music, literature, or architecture. And who says these forms have to be distinct?

"The creative act brings to life, in its various forms, an infinity of experiences to anyone willing to accept it," Harry says.

Pietro likes this line so much that he asks Harry to repeat it. Pietro writes it down. The sentence seems at once so concrete, such a solid expression of an idea, and yet exasperatingly ephemeral. If he doesn't write it down, it might float away and then he could never recapture it. Then again, losing the fear of not being able to recapture an idea is part of the process. Pietro can't be afraid of losing an idea, because he can always find it again within himself whenever he needs to.

Harry Wentz is a man full of life. Many men who have faced death are. Pietro always knew he might die in the Great War, but Harry had been told to his face, by doctors, that he had only a couple years to live. Harry was young then, only in his twenties. So, Harry used every dime he had to take a trip to Paris—perhaps that's what had given him the spirit of Rimbaud. He vowed to live it up in the City of Lights until the darkness surrounded him. But it never did.

Harry is around fifty now, as far as Pietro can tell, because Harry's age sometimes seems as ephemeral as the lines he spouts. Perhaps Harry did a deal with the devil. Or perhaps the city that stripped Rimbaud of his poetry redistributed it into Harry. Whatever it is, whatever energy floats through the air as Harry speaks, Pietro perceives it. Harry has helped Pietro harness it, taught him how to conceive of art as integral to, and inextricable from, its surroundings. How color can enhance or detract from its relation to form, and how those two things synthesize to create a third thing, something that is neither form nor color, but rather something unique in the mind of the observer.

In the mind of . . . Pietro taps into his well, remembering Marinetti. This is the lesson that madman was trying to teach him as well. Pietro's skin tingles. It's curious, isn't it? The lessons you're taught over and over until you finally realize how right they are. Like a mantra, these lessons fold on top of one another until you can see past them, past the problem, toward the solution. And there's no use shooting the messenger if you don't learn the lesson the first time, especially with someone like Marinetti, because that messenger will shoot back.

Two different messengers. And now two years in Portland.

But has he learned his lesson? Pietro thinks he has. He's learned how important it is to see a work of art as a whole, not as a sum of its constituent parts. Not to simply describe the surface, but to dig deeper and uncover what lies underneath. It's a problem of effortless Awareness. It's something hard to comprehend because it's the thing we think we're already doing all the time, on the surface, in our brains. But Awareness with a capital A is something much deeper, something much harder to tap into unless you slow down and concentrate on it, tap into that deep well inside you and bring forth the spring. "Sense the spring . . . Sense the spring . . ." It's a phrase worth remembering.

Pietro's English has only gotten better, and now, with the accumulation of all this new art-speak, Pietro appears and sounds like a new man. He's not just drinking from a fountain of wisdom; he's able to spout that wisdom out.

"Let's celebrate," Mr. Greene announces as he pats Pietro on the back after another successful night of class. "I'm having a party at my place tonight. Now, actually. And we mustn't be late."

Pietro grins. He's grown fond of Mr. Greene over these past two years. Mr. Greene's brusque demeanor is no longer something to fear, but something rather dear. Pietro doesn't even mind that when they show up at his place, the first time Pietro has ever been to his apartment, Mr. Greene asks Pietro to help him prepare for the party. "Arrange the drinks while I decorate. And give it a nice tableau."

By now, Pietro should know that for Mr. Greene, even the drinks need to put on a show.

Mr. Greene ducks into the bedroom and returns a minute later dressed in a kimono. "What do you think?" he asks.

"I—uh, is that Japanese?"

"Yes, and *from* Japan, actually, not just made in one of the local shops." Mr. Greene does a quick spin.

"You look marvelous," Pietro says. "You're the only one in the office who doesn't wear a smock, and I think . . . the only one who could pull off wearing that."

Ring. Ring. The doorbell and Mr. Greene almost burst with excitement. But before Mr. Greene opens the door, he turns to Pietro and says, "Tonight, call me Charlie. Everyone else will."

A gaggle of men enter the apartment and whirl around Charlie as he twirls in the center of them.

"Charlie!"

"Charlie, you look dashing!"

"Don't tell me that's new!"

There's something decidedly different about Mr. Greene tonight. And there's something decidedly different about the men at Mr. Greene's party. Perhaps what's most conspicuous, though, has nothing to do with them, but with something the party lacks: women.

Gaggle after gaggle of men enter the apartment, all cackling and crowing about Charlie's kimono. Gaggle is the right word for a group of men, isn't it? Pietro still struggles with words sometimes, but that seems like the right word, even if it isn't, at least for these men.

Then again, sometimes words do matter. And although Pietro likes to think he gained a mastery of the language, he can't quite piece together what's going on when, suddenly, red and blue lights flash outside the apartment.

Perhaps it's the alcohol, but Pietro can't understand what's going on. Yes, he is at a party, and yes, everyone has been drinking. But unlike the officers who raided the speakeasy, these officers don't seem as concerned about the liquor as they do about the younger men in attendance.

To some people, Pietro is still relatively new to Portland, especially as a foreigner, but these young men seem relatively new to adulthood. He heard them talking about a football team and thought they were talking about the University of Oregon, but it turns out they were talking about their high school team, which they still play for.

"He's not with us. He's not a part of this," Charlie says as he points at Pietro. "You should let him go. He's Italian, and he probably doesn't even understand what's going on."

It's the truth. Pietro had a hard time understanding some of the more creative lingo the men used tonight, and while he knows what Charlie is saying now, Pietro knows better than to question him, especially when Charlie is staring him down.

"Please, let him leave," Charlie implores the cops.

"Go on. Get out of here," one of the cops says.

Slowly, silently, Pietro exits Charlie's apartment. He'll ask Charlie about what happened tomorrow at the office. Pietro won't be drunk then, so maybe he'll understand better.

But tomorrow never comes. From what Pietro can gather over the next week, Charlie wasn't jailed for inviting teenagers to his house party, but the cops weren't too kindly about letting him stay out of jail either. Instead of prosecuting him, they gave him the opportunity to gather his things and skip town. No moving trucks. No goodbyes. Just take anything he can carry as long as he leaves town and never comes back.

"Charlie's departure is more like a death." That's the way Eddie describes it when he returns from Italy, only to find he'll never see Charlie again. "We were different men in a lot of ways," Eddie continues, "but similar in the ones that mattered."

Eddie returned from Italy full of new experiences. And full of dread. When a dog is sick, it'll often wander off and lay itself to rest in some quiet, hidden corner. But Eddie was engulfed with the strong desire to return to Portland, to lay himself to rest in the city he knew best.

Bright's disease. Such a funny name for something that can kill you. At least that's what Eddie used to say. A smile creeps across Pietro's cheek as he sits at Eddie's funeral, remembering him fondly, but he can't bring himself to laugh.

Unfortunately, lessons aren't the only things that can repeat themselves. One loss can follow another, but it's harder to cipher what you're supposed to learn from them.

Two men. Two deaths, one literal, and one figurative. In two years. Both had been mentors to Pietro in their own way. A set of father figures in place of the one he left behind in Italy.

How can you say goodbye to someone who's transformed your life? While they may have been in his life only temporarily, Pietro's reverence for Eddie and Charles is eternal.

As Pietro says goodbye to them, he discovers a letter from his real father. Oddly enough, it's in his mother's handwriting.

"Your father is about to undergo surgery . . ." the letter starts, "and he might not make it."

Chapter Thirteen

IT'S ALL A BIT FOGGY

How did he get here?

The ship. Yes, that's right. Pietro is sailing back to Italy on the same ocean liner that brought him to America. But this time, he didn't pack any suits. Rather than promenading around the promenade, Pietro mostly stays in his room, half out of worry for his father and half out of studiousness. Charles is gone, now Eddie, and perhaps his father as well.

Screech. Squeal. The deck chairs keel. The only available stateroom was right below the promenade deck. There's turbulence on the sea this time of year, which causes the deck chairs to flip over every now and again. And even when they're not flipping over, someone's always rearranging them. It makes it hard to study.

The early morning, though, is when the deck chairs move the most. That's when the ship attendants get them ready for the day. It's so loud. Pietro can't stay in his room. It's the only time of day he allows himself to venture out.

This is the only time of day others aren't parading around

the ship. So, there's less chance of running into anyone and striking up a conversation. Conversations lead to dinners, and dinners are just a waste of time.

But in the early morning, when the beating overhead overwhelms him, Pietro takes it as an opportunity to stretch his legs. He wishes he could run, but on this ship all one can get is a brisk walk or a light jog. There's nowhere to run.

Death can bring many things, but one of the most important in the long run is opportunity. The men at his firm will all shift around in their roles due to these departures, and Pietro might be given an opportunity to advance. He graduated from tracing other people's designs long ago. He's been able to do a few of his own, but because his architecture firm is a group environment, the credit often goes to the team and not to him. *That's fine. That's just the way it goes*, Pietro consoles himself. It will all be different once he passes the state licensing exam and becomes an architect in his own right.

By now, Pietro is certain he knows what he needs to do. He needs to wake up at four in the morning every day until the day of the test. That's what he's done in the past, and that's what he knows works. The only problem is that he has trouble keeping track of time. He has trouble keeping the worry about his father out of his mind. He has trouble keeping the pain of losing two other men in his life out of his heart.

Beat. Beat. Pietro's heart races as he runs down the street and bursts into his parent's house.

"Where's Father?" Pietro asks his mother.

"Oh, good. You came!" Pietro's father interjects, walking in the door behind him. "I'm glad I finished my walk early."

"Your walk? I thought you were going to die!"

"Yes, but I didn't. And now I'm better."

Pietro can't quite recall what he does after that. No, the rage takes care of that. All better? His father had said he was dying. Pietro came all the way back here, expecting him to be on his deathbed, and now he's going for walks like nothing happened.

Pietro boards the next ship back to America. But this one is a different vessel. Not as lavish as the *Conte Rosso*, but much more economical. To Pietro, it doesn't matter. He isn't planning to partake in its amenities. No, he came back to Italy under false pretenses. His father always had a flair for the dramatic, and while Pietro is relieved he's alive, he can't handle returning to Italy without achieving the success he wants for himself. How could he have explained to his parents that he was just working in an office, after all these years? How could he explain that he's trying to make something of himself when he has nothing to show for it?

The sun rises early over the sea. There are no buildings to block it. Pietro rises early as well, to imagine the buildings he'll design. He's focused on his own rise more than the sun's.

Which is all well and good but, again, how did he get here? Pietro remembers sailing on the ship. But now he's here, in the courtyard of the Fogg Art Museum in Cambridge, Massachusetts, on the campus of Harvard University. Pietro remembers reading about the museum in *Architectural Forum* magazine. But that doesn't explain it.

Although Pietro is in Massachusetts, he could just as well be in Italy. Montepulciano, Italy, to be exact. The museum was modeled after the facade of a house built in the sixteenth century. Or at least its courtyard was.

The house at the church of San Biagio in Montepulciano was built by Antonio da San Gallo the Elder, so, really, his name should be on this museum as much as Fogg's, alongside the architects Coolidge, Shepley, Bulfinch, and Abbott.

It is a lovely courtyard. The arches are well placed, giving the galleries a sense of exploration. But it needs more light. When Pietro designs a museum, it will have more light. And that's when Pietro remembers why he's here. He wanted to take a quick break from his studies before he boarded the train back to Portland, and he wanted to see what the fuss was all about with this new museum.

And now he's taking a break from exploring the museum to design his own. Pietro occupies a bench in the courtyard, while another courtyard occupies his mind. Pietro's eyes search up to the ceiling and back down to his sketch. A skylight. His museum will have a skylight. But skylights can be expensive. And the light they produce can be rather harsh. So, what if he installed the skylight at a slant, so the sun streams in through the side instead of directly to the ground? Yes, that could work.

After a while, Pietro stops to inspect his sketch. It's simpler than most museums. Maybe more of a gallery—not quite a museum on its own, but perhaps part of one. It looks a bit like the Fogg, but it's more modern, not constrained by the style of the past.

Pietro shuts his sketchbook. That was a pleasant break, but now it's time to get back to his proper work: studying for his licensing exam.

Town after town whips past as Pietro flips through page after page. It's all becoming a bit of a blur: the walls, the arches, the acronyms, the codes. It's all a big, Brobdingnagian ball in his brain. Somehow it all seems to make more sense after he takes a nap. But that's all he can give himself. There is no sleeping, not really. There is no more four o'clock in the morning, no wake-up time. Every time is wake-up time, time to keep studying.

Pietro wrote ahead before he left Italy to schedule his test immediately upon his return. And he is only going to arrive just in time. His train is scheduled to arrive in the morning, and his test is that afternoon. It is the most perverted welcome-back party one could imagine, but the outcome will hopefully lead to something hospitable. He can't fail again, like he did the Cornell placement test. Pietro must pass.

Pietro can't remember much about the test itself. All he can remember is his fingers flying across the page.

But, apparently, he recalled some things while taking the test, because not only does he pass with flying colors, but he receives the highest score of anyone who takes the test that year. Take that, Cornell.

"We knew you had it in you!" Pietro's coworker says as he slaps him on the back. The entire firm celebrates along with Pietro when he receives the news. The slap reverberates through Pietro's body like an earthquake, shaking loose the pent-up energy he's been storing, and shaking loose the sketchbook in his hand. It tumbles to the floor, opening up to the sketch Pietro made in the courtyard of the Fogg.

"What do we have here?" a coworker asks. "Looks like an art museum."

"Or a gallery," another pipes in.

"Too bad they're already giving that new wing to Jamieson Parker."

"Who? What wing?" Pietro asks.

"The Portland Art Museum. They're commissioning a new wing."

Pietro scans the sketch and takes stock of this newfound awareness inside of him, this confidence after passing the licensing exam. There's only one question worth asking. "Have they made their final decision yet?"

"I don't think so, but I know they've already commissioned some designs from him."

"Good," Pietro says as he storms out of the office. He knows where the Portland Art Museum is. The only thing he doesn't know is whom he should talk to once he arrives.

"Who's in charge of commissioning the new wing?" Pietro asks a guard at the entrance.

After a few minutes of confused wrangling, a sturdy woman clacks her way across a gallery over to Pietro. "Yes, what is this about?"

"Who are you?" Pietro asks her.

"I'm Anna Crocker, curator of the museum," she responds, tapping her foot, pretending Pietro is a bug underneath her shoe. "So I'll ask you again: what is this about?"

Pietro inhales. It's the first time he's about to say these words and he can already tell how sweet they're going to taste on his lips. "I'm an architect," Pietro whispers before speaking up, "I'm an architect, and I have a design I think you should consider for your new wing."

He opens up his sketchbook and shows it to her.

"You think you can just walk in here, show me some sketch, and we're going to stop everything and give you the commission?"

"I, uh—"

"We've already been working with Mr. Parker, Mr.—I didn't get your name."

"Belluschi. Pietro Belluschi."

"Well, yes, we're already looking at designs by Mr. Parker. He's been a member of the board for quite some time already. And, well . . ." Anna pauses, choosing her next words carefully. "I'm sure Mr. Parker will amend his designs soon in order to deliver the most desirable experience for our visitors."

Pietro's eyes glow. "What do you want the museum to feel like?"

"I—I'm sorry," Anna says. "I'm not quite sure what you mean."

"What emotions do you want to evoke when people enter the space? Do you want the gallery to be a feature, a work of art itself? Or do you want it to blend into the background? What would be the best way the wing could enhance the work *you* do?"

Anna shifts, checks out Pietro's sketch one more time. "These are, uh, excellent questions, Mr. . . ."

"Belluschi."

"Yes. Well, I'm sorry. I have a certain sense of how to answer your questions. I'm just . . . pleased you're asking them. Mr. Parker doesn't—well, he is a lovely man, but he can be rather set in his ways."

Pietro has had his head buried in a book for so long, he almost forgot he knows how to read people. And if he can tell anything by looking at Anna, he can tell there's an opening, an opportunity here.

Pietro points at his sketch, then closes his sketchbook. "It might not be exactly what you're looking for yet, but I can promise you I'll listen to everything you need and deliver something that you, Portland, and the world can be proud of. What do you think?"

Anna eyes Pietro. He's still rather young, unpolished. But there's something there, something in his rough stone exterior . . . Michelangelo said he could see into a slab of stone and unlock its true potential. Perhaps this time, it's Anna who has the key.

"I think we should continue this conversation in my office," Anna replies.

Chapter Fourteen

IT ALL COMES CRASHING DOWN

It crashed. Smashed. All of Pietro's hopes . . . dashed.

Pietro sits across from Anna Crocker in her office. Her eyes look red and puffy, like she's been crying. A lot of people have been crying nowadays. The stock market wiped out fortunes, but even for those less well inclined, it wiped out their prospects.

The roaring twenties ended with a scream for help. In a former life, Anna had been the secretary to a banker who founded the museum, so she understands what it's been like down at the banks. It was like a giant tsunami attacked the shore, sucking everything it could into the ocean.

But don't think Anna got her job as curator because of her proximity to one of the museum's founders. She graduated from the Art Students League in New York. Then she went to Europe, not just touring the museums and galleries around the continent like any other artist, but interviewing museum directors to see how they command their ships, determining what she would do differently and what tactics she could bring back to Portland.

Pietro sits across from a woman twenty years into her tenure as curator, although *director* might be a more fitting title because she not only arranges the art on the walls, but directs everything within them.

Pietro's launchpad was supposed to be her capstone, a crowning achievement to her career. "But it's all come crashing down," Anna says.

Pietro and Anna worked together on the design for the new wing. Pietro tried to distill her years of experience into the design. "Light. Some people might think the most important thing in a gallery is space, but it's really the light that draws you in," Pietro remembers Anna saying at their first design meeting. Pietro took the idea to heart. He made light the fundamental theme that drove his design.

His new wing was to comprise an entrance, a sculpture court, and galleries. The upper floor would have paintings. To make sure they were well lit, Pietro surrounded the ceiling with banks of monitor windows. He softened the light, though, by adding a five-foot cove beneath the windows to create a sunny, inviting glow inside the galleries instead of a harsh glare. Squint your eyes and you can see it's a version of the slanted skylights Pietro sketched in the Fogg.

Anna brings Pietro's design to C. F. Adams, the chairperson of the building committee, and extolls the virtue of Pietro's design. Ostensibly, she seeks his guidance and favor before bringing it to the rest of the board, who she anticipates will have some reservations about the design. And although they might be a board, they definitely won't be bored. The design is fresh, like the air in Portland. And Anna likes it, which is all the board really needs. And why not? She is a great curator and everything goes well. Until it doesn't.

"The board is just a little cautious about choosing a design from an untested architect in these troubling times," Anna says diplomatically.

Pietro knows society is unraveling, but now, apparently, so is his career. His firm recently promoted him to head of the design department, the same position Charles Greene used to occupy, because Pietro single-handedly brought this new project to their firm. But now that it's being taken away from him, will the promotion be as well?

Pietro's eyes lose focus like he's under a spell. What's he going to do?

Anna's face pinches. "They've suggested I go ask Frank Lloyd Wright if he'd be interested in designing the wing when he's over at the university for his lecture."

Pietro bites his bottom lip. Frank Lloyd Wright could walk into any architecture firm and steal any project he wanted. Perhaps that's why he goes on his lecture tours—or perhaps Pietro should call them hunting expeditions. But, luckily, Pietro hasn't heard of him doing anything like that before. Would Anna even be interested in bringing on Wright if she could?

"But I would never do that," Anna continues, assuaging Pietro's fear. "Plus, I don't think we can afford him."

Indeed, the wing's $125,000 budget might not even cover Wright's fees. Or so Pietro assumes Wright's ego would demand.

"Ladies and gentlemen, I don't think humility is a very becoming state for me," Wright says at the beginning of his lecture to a few dozen students, assembled academics, and various interlopers such as Anna and Pietro.

Pietro now sits next to Anna instead of across from her. The rest of Wright's speech deals with his belief in developing architecture in harmony with the surrounding environment. It must feel organic, created in combination with nature to serve humanity. Or at least that's what Pietro believes the speech is about. He tunes in and out, catching snippets of words. It doesn't really matter what Wright says during his lecture. It matters what he says after it. Will Anna really ask Wright to design the museum? Would he actually say yes?

Pietro circles Wright after his lecture. Everyone's pecking at him, begging for their brief moment before he turns his attention to someone else. Vultures. That's what vultures do—circle their prey, hoping there's enough for them to eat.

"Mr. Wright, I'm Anna Crocker, curator of the Portland Museum of Art, and, well, I'm wondering if you might be interested in designing a new wing for us."

Wright raises his eyebrow. "A new wing? Why not a whole museum?"

"That's not quite in our budget."

"What is your budget?"

"Umm . . ." Anna looks around.

By now, Pietro has spent enough time with Anna to know she's not comfortable answering that question out loud, so he steps in and hands her his sketchbook. "Go ahead. Write it down."

Anna scribbles the number on a sheet of paper and hands it to Wright. "That's for the entire project."

Wright cackles, then at least has the decency to change it to a chortle. "I guess if you were interested in adding a few rooms, but a whole wing?" Wright's eyes shift to the side. He blinks. His nose wrinkles. Then his eyes land on Pietro's sketchbook. "Hand me a piece of paper."

Pietro rips out a sheet.

"Now, if I were designing a museum, I'd want it to look something like this . . ." Wright says as he sketches something that looks like the world's most squat tornado, or a flattened corkscrew. "People could start at one point and walk all the way up or down, never stopping."

"But then wouldn't people notice the architecture more than the art?" Pietro asks.

"That's the whole point, isn't it? To create art that rivals theirs? Something worthy enough to house their masterpieces?"

Anna looks back and forth between the men, wondering when they'll pull out their yardsticks. "Your design is quite . . . ambitious, Mr. Wright. It's unfortunate that we'd never be able to afford it."

"But they can afford something like this," Pietro says, unfurling his design on a nearby desk.

Wright perches over the design, looking down on it like a hawk waiting for the right time to strike. But he doesn't. "I think your plan is straightforward," he starts, "and sensible. That exterior, though. That would at least mark an advantage in culture for Portland. I see a bit of the Fogg in it, but it's not a British architect's idea of what Italian architecture used to be. It's . . . here, in Portland, and not someplace else. I like it."

Pietro steps forward, knowing it's time to strike. "Would you do us a favor and tell other people that? Specifically, the museum's board of directors?"

Wright nods. But he does a lot more when he's summoned in front of C. F. Adams and the rest of the board.

"You don't want to go in the wrong direction, do you?" Wright says, really laying into them. "You're not a history museum, are you? No, you house art. Art that inspires what humanity can achieve. You don't want to look to the past. You must look to the future. Use Mr. Belluschi's design, unless you'd like to take Portland in the wrong direction."

Wright pauses for their applause, which comes quickly.

Pietro can't tell if the board really believes in what Wright is saying or if they're simply starstruck, but what does that matter if it gets him his first major commission?

"How can I ever repay you?" Pietro asks him.

"Repay me?" Wright responds with a cocked eyebrow. "I don't need your help, but you know what? Find someone who does."

Chapter Fifteen

SCRAPING THE SKY

"Should there be a ribbon?" Pietro asks Anna Crocker at the opening ceremony for the Ayer Wing, the newly christened addition to the Portland Art Museum. Wright's speech was all the board needed to hear in order to back Pietro's design.

Pietro has heard ribbon-cutting ceremonies were becoming more popular in America. He doesn't remember who told him, but the first one might have been for a Louisiana railroad in the nineteenth century. Leave it to the Americans to invent a novel way to promote themselves.

Unfortunately, there's no ribbon at this opening ceremony, but there are two different cakes, one with frosting and one with something much sweeter.

Ralph Cake, a man with a penchant for suits that rivals Pietro's, walks up to him. "So, what's next, young man?"

Young man? Pietro has met Cake a few times, so he bristles at the fact that he doesn't remember his name. Cake was a longtime client of the A. E. Doyle architecture firm. He is the president of the Equitable Savings and Loan Association, and he knows exactly what is coming next: nothing. The Depression cleared out most of Pietro's firm's portfolio.

"I'm Pietro Belluschi, sir. I designed this wing."

"I know," Cake replies. "That's why I'm talking to you. Starting to make a name for yourself, aren't you?"

Pietro blushes. He doesn't know what to say. He heard his design for the museum has been traveling around the country a bit, but he hasn't quite learned how to deal with his newfound popularity. "Thank you, sir. I—"

"Do you know the story of Icarus?" Cake interjects.

"Yes," Pietro responds. "The man who flew too close to the sun."

"Mankind itself has been flying too close to the sun these days. That's what led to the Depression," Mr. Cake says solemnly, but then a smile creeps across his cheek. "Want to see how close you can get? I'd like to commission a skyscraper from you."

Pietro sucks in a quick breath. His eyes widen. He can't believe it. It's too good to be true, but before he can question Cake's motives, Pietro finds himself outfitted with wings. No longer does he have to travel cross-country on a train. No, now he's flying first class.

Despite the Depression, Cake wants to build a skyscraper in Manhattan. And he wants Pietro, a rising star in architecture, to design it.

Chicago. Philadelphia. Each city's skyline stretches to the heavens, but each city has another looming on the horizon: New York. No other city can boast as many skyscrapers. No other city can toast as many Icaruses. It's true that with the Depression, the city has shrunk into a deep pit of despair. So, Cake seeks to escape it in the air.

Pietro tours Manhattan with Cake, soaking in the current developments in skyscraper design, hoping Pietro can top them all. The Chrysler Building was the world's tallest building for eleven months until the Empire State Building overtook it. Its design splintered the sky and split people's opinions. Some people love the Chrysler Building's art deco design. Others see it as a monstrosity, but then again, that always seems to happen when something truly new pierces a city's skyline.

The writer Guy de Maupassant famously ate lunch underneath the Eiffel Tower every day because it was the only place in Paris where he couldn't see his "iron arch nemesis," what he derisively called the tower. Writers are often overly dramatic, prone to flights of fancy. And while it's true that not everyone in Paris loves the Eiffel Tower, it has become an indelible symbol of the city.

Pietro wants to create his own symbol, something that will stand out in New York regardless of its initial reception. To do that, he and Cake will have to partner with an East Coast firm, for geographical proximity, if not architectural prowess.

"Scotch or whiskey?" It's the question they always ask Pietro when he visits these firms. If Pietro drank at all these meetings, he'd become a drunk. Everyone can sense the end of Prohibition, so they've stopped the pretense, but Pietro doesn't want the stink of alcohol on him. He already smells too much like the West Coast for their liking.

Pietro wants these architectural firms to schmooze him with

their logistical expertise instead of their booze. He doesn't want them to feel like they can pull anything over on him just because he hasn't worked on the East Coast before.

Some firms trot out even more nefarious methods of getting Pietro's attention, trying to ply him with women, hoping he'll let his guard down if they can get into his pants.

At one firm, one woman does catch his eye, but not because she's trying to gain his attention. It's because she's paying him no mind. Usually, the secretaries at these firms are quite attentive, or at least kind, but in this one, she doesn't even acknowledge Pietro when he enters. She keeps her head buried in the most recent edition of *Architectural Forum.*

Clean lines. High ceilings. Ample light. Pietro identifies the designs she's looking at from across the room. "Frank Lloyd Wright, hm? You know, I've met the man."

"You have?" she asks, now giving Pietro her full attention. "Tell me, is he actually flesh and blood? Sometimes I can't believe he's real."

"He's the reason I'm standing here, if that answers your question."

"What do you mean?"

"He helped me get my first big commission."

"And what did he get out of it?"

Pietro squints. What a curious question. "Well, I guess he did it out of the goodness of his heart, although he did ask me to pass on the favor."

The secretary is confused. "So, he got *nothing* out of it?" She sighs. "Oh, well, that's disappointing. I guess we all have our flaws."

Pietro smiles. He knows he should remind her he's here for an appointment, but he'd rather know more about this interesting creature. "Your accent, is that Russian?"

"And you're Italian, right?" she says, responding with a question.

"What's your name?"

"Ayn. Ayn Rand."

"Ayn?" Pietro drawls, trying to sound it out.

"Rhymes with 'mine,'" she responds. How fitting.

"You don't seem the secretarial type. If you don't mind me saying so."

"I'd be offended if you did," Ayn says flatly. "I'm only working here to soak up information for a novel I'm working on."

"You're a writer?"

Ayn puffs up. "Cecil B. DeMille in Hollywood says I am, if you don't believe me."

"Don't worry. I do," Pietro says with a smile. "What's your novel about?"

"Well, I must figure that out now that you've informed me Mr. Wright is flawed. Why does every man have to have a flaw? Can't there be one man without any?"

Pietro leans in to commiserate. "I love his work, but I want to design buildings that are . . . more functional."

"Functional?" Ayn groans. "So, you want to fit in." It's not a question; it's an accusation.

"I don't care if people like it or not, if that's what you're getting at. This skyscraper I'm designing, if your firm is lucky enough to get it, will become a landmark. If not today or in my lifetime, then eventually, when people come to their senses. But yes, form follows function. If you're not designing a building with its function in mind, then you might as well be building sandcastles, because the sands of time will sweep it away."

Ayn purses her lips, considering Pietro's point.

"Have you asked Mr. Belluschi if he wants a drink?" Ayn's boss asks her as he bounds into the lobby. "I'm sorry if she kept you waiting."

"Actually, she kept me entertained," Pietro responds. "In fact, I'd like to partner with your firm, on one condition."

"What is that?" Ayn asks before her boss can.

"That you give this woman access to anything she needs for her novel." Pietro grins, glad to have found someone to pass on Wright's good grace. But when he looks at Ayn's face, she doesn't seem pleased. She seems nonplussed, disappointed somehow.

"Only take his offer if it's what's best for you," Ayn commands her boss. "What I need should have no bearing on your consideration."

"Don't worry. It doesn't," her boss responds as he extends his hand to Pietro. "You have a deal."

Chapter Sixteen

I, PIETRO

Never regret thy fall,
O Icarus of the fearless flight,
For the greatest tragedy of them all
Is never to feel the burning light.

Pietro believes this quote belongs to Oscar Wilde, but he can't find it in any of Wilde's published works. It doesn't seem to matter, though. Nothing seems to matter these days. The plans for Pietro's skyscraper evaporated as if they had been made of wax. That's a curious thing, isn't it—that we see Icarus as the incarnation of hubris, when his story should just be a warning to engineers to choose the right material.

Pietro thought he'd build his skyscraper out of steel. Would it have gone forward if he chose brick instead? Pietro couldn't have built so high, but would that have stopped Cake from cancelling the project? Even Cake can't outrun the Depression. The economy didn't dip, it cratered. And, similar to the experience of the last lingering dinosaurs, the impact was cataclysmic, even if they thought they could survive it.

There's no work in Pietro's firm, no commissions. There's no work anywhere. Everything is scarce, including hope. Maybe that's why Oregon is having a competition. The competition isn't about deciding on a dome as much as it is about giving the various architectural firms something to do.

Similar to Brunelleschi's dome in Florence, the Oregon State Legislature is having a competition to redesign the dome of the Oregon State Capitol. The original capitol burned down in 1855. Then the dome's second iteration suffered the same fate in 1935. It was a 180-foot dome designed in the classical fashion. *Is that what they want again, or do they want something more modern?* Pietro wonders.

Normally, Pietro would like to sit the commissioners down and discuss their needs, so he wouldn't waste his time. But now, all he and the skeleton crew left in his office have is time.

"What do we do?"

"Should we style it on the capitol dome in DC?"

"Maybe something more avant-garde?"

"Or cheap! They're probably just going to choose the cheapest one. That's what everyone else is doing, anyway."

These are the conversations Pietro has with his staff. Conversations turn to arguments, turn to reconciliation, turn to ideation. They mull over their proposal, hoping it's not dull. While Pietro would like to get his architecture career back on track, he knows this project is much more important than that.

It's the only thing that could keep everyone in his office afloat as well.

"We don't have to choose," Pietro realizes. "Traditional or modern—it doesn't matter. We'll design both, and maybe one in between, and let them choose. We don't have to figure out what they want. We just have to submit proposals for anything they *could* want, then let them choose ours."

There's a long pause after Pietro lays out this plan. It'll be three times the work, but if they don't do it, there's nothing in their pipeline after that. And that means there will be nothing on their dinner tables. And, boy, are they hungry.

Pietro leads the staff, pulling all-nighters and delivering all three designs, just like he outlined. There is the traditional, pedimented, classical dome. There is a modern one without a dome, but rather a central tower similar to a skyscraper. And then there's one in between those two, just in case the committee members can't make up their minds. Even though Pietro has never entered a competition before, he thinks he knows what's in store. Victory. There's no way they won't choose one of his team's designs.

One. Two. Three. One. Two. Three.

It's not just the number of proposals they submitted; it's the beat Pietro keeps pounding with his fist against his leg as he and his staff await the announcement about the winner of the Oregon State Capitol competition.

A thumbtack pierces the paper as a committee member

posts the announcement at the capitol, but it might as well be piercing Pietro's heart. Perhaps it's God getting back at Pietro for Cake commissioning him instead of a New York City architect to design a Manhattan skyscraper, because now the New York City architects are coming to Oregon. Pietro and his team lose the competition to the New York architects Francis Keally and Trowbridge & Livingston.

"It looks just like our one . . . our one in between!" Pietro screams when he sees the winning design. "It's a sort of cylindrical dome. Reminiscent of a classical one, but unmistakably modern."

Now, not only is the economy depressed, but Pietro is too.

The sea slapping against the hull feels like a slap across his face.

There's nothing in America for Pietro, at least at the moment, so he returns to Rome, but he doesn't return home. If he stayed with his parents, he'd be a failure. The apocalypse is no excuse for being eclipsed. Other architects got work, so it's his fault.

Pietro roams about Rome, excavating the simpler times of his youth. He's aimless until he recalls something his father told him on one of their many walks: "You must find your muses."

So, Pietro goes back to the same bookstore where he once searched for Rimbaud.

There. In the window sits a stack of red-cloth books with an odd assortment of initials on the binding. *I, Claudius* by R. Graves. Or at least it looks like initials. The title seems to have a comma in it, not a period. Pietro spots a lamp insignia on the bookplate along with the words *Ex Libris*. Apparently, there was an overprint of library copies and this shop is selling the surplus. The book was discounted, and once he starts reading, Pietro can tell why. This book wasn't written by R. Graves. That's a misprint on the cover; Claudius wrote the book himself. This is just a translation. So why was R. Graves's name on the spine? Maybe he translated it?

"Can you imagine writing an entire novel using autobiographical style?" a man asks Pietro, holding a copy of the same book.

"I can, because it *is* an autobiography," Pietro corrects.

"But it's not," the man rectifies. "Graves just wrote it that way, as if Claudius had written his own autobiography. But it's all Graves."

"That seems silly. Why would he do that?"

"To get us into the mind of the character, I suppose."

Pietro sets the book down. "There are better ways to do that than this, producing what is basically a fake historical document."

The man picks up another copy and hands it to Pietro. "Do yourself a favor," he says, "and get over it."

The man walks away, leaving Pietro with the book in his hand and something to consider.

He finds a chair in the corner of the store. It's a library copy of a book, so he may as well treat this bookstore like a library, he figures.

It only takes a chapter, but then Pietro knows he can't spend any more time reading *I, Claudius* in this store.

Before, with the man, Pietro had a short fuse. But now, he's found it. His muse.

Pietro tracks down the locations mentioned in the book as soon as he comes across them on the page. The Apollo Library on the Palatine Hill. That's close to the Forum, near the crumbling edifices. It's where Claudius started writing his book. Maybe it's where Graves started as well?

Pietro wades through the former floodplain of the Tiber River to the Ara Pacis. Is this the altar Claudius describes in the book, the one built by Augustus? The one whose unveiling caused Claudius's mother to go into shock, leading to his premature birth?

Nowadays, the altar is under thirteen feet of silt, the slow shifting of the Tiber River burying this secret, so it's a little hard to tell. Even so, Pietro wants to be as close to Claudius's story as he can. He wants to reach out and touch the world he's reading about.

He walks to Ostia near the sea, idling away the hours nestled between the seats in the open-air *Teatro di Ostia.* Pietro even travels to Campania. He hikes Mount Gaurus near Naples, then explores the Temple of Jupiter in Rome and the Cave of the Sibyl in Cumae. Is this the Sibyl whom Claudius visits in her "cliff cavern on Mount Gaurus"?

As Pietro approaches the peak, he can't help but think Graves is peaking as well. Rather, that Graves has achieved the apex of how an author can approach character, at least in autobiographical style. The writing, from Claudius's point of view, is so engrossing. It's like Pietro is walking in Claudius's shoes himself. Perhaps that's why he started on this journey in the first place. Pietro's mind convinced his feet to walk in Claudius's footsteps.

In Rome, there are so many gods, so many statues to them. But where are the statues to Claudius? Where can Pietro idolize him? Claudius is a man who overcame his setbacks and still achieved greatness, becoming emperor, etching his name in the annals of history, even though everyone wrote him off.

The more Pietro learns about Claudius, the more he wants to learn about the man behind the mask. Pietro discovers that Graves went straight from school to the Great War, just like Pietro did, and became a captain in the Royal Welch Fusiliers.

Pietro empathizes with the pain Graves put into the novel. The fear of being forgotten. The fear of serving for years and not living up to your potential. The fear of not being recognized for what you have to offer. But just like Claudius, Pietro will overcome this. This depression. This Depression. This never-ending session of cessation. It will be Pietro's new obsession.

The goal: ascension.

No more indiscretion.

Only forward progression.

Chapter Seventeen

HELEN OF PORTLAND

"I do not think it is natural for an ordinary man to live long without a woman."

—Tiberius Claudius Drusus Nero Germanicus,
via Robert Graves

Of course Pietro thinks about women. Sometimes they're all he can think about. But he has never been calculated about it. He has never thought about women in the way men do when marriage is part of the equation.

Dating seems just as perilous as marriage. What if he makes the wrong choice? What if he wastes time on one woman while losing out on another?

Pietro has nothing but time when he returns to Portland. What he doesn't have is money or a place to live, which means he probably won't have a girlfriend either.

"Room for rent." It's odd that such a simple sign would lead to such an important encounter.

Whenever Pietro thinks of love, he often thinks of Helen of

Troy. Now *that's* a story about love. Or at least a story about how it can go wrong.

When many people think of her, they think of her beauty. "Was this the face that launched a thousand ships?" Christopher Marlowe wrote in 1604. Pietro can't help but wonder, *Could anyone really possess such beauty, even if they were a demigod like Helen of Troy? And even if they did, is beauty something you can possess, or is it something that possesses others?*

Pietro follows the "Room for rent" sign up a rickety set of stairs to a small apartment and finds his own Helen waiting for him, albeit under a different set of circumstances.

Pietro stands transfixed. A woman with slicked-back hair, severe brows, and a hard stare walks up to him, looking like Marlene Dietrich playing Helen of Troy. "Are you here to see the apartment?" she asks.

Pietro doesn't answer. There are no thoughts running through his head. Rather, they hover above his body. He stands there still, his heart stops, like he's dead, although he's never felt more alive. Later, Pietro will realize this out-of-body experience answers his earlier question. *Yes, it's the beauty that does the possessing.*

While the woman's stare might be hard, her eyes are soft, inviting. "It isn't much to see, but let me show you around."

She spins and takes in the small space. It is a bachelor apartment in the truest sense. One room with an attached bath. No one else would live there except a man who has nowhere else to go.

"Well, there isn't that much to show," she says. "But if

you take the place, I'll help you spruce it up with some art, or maybe . . ." Her hand gestures to the only large wall. "Maybe a tapestry here. That would look lovely."

"Nothing could look lovely in here with you standing beside it," Pietro spouts. They're the first words he's spoken to her, which is both pathetic and prophetic.

"Don't think you can sweet-talk me to get a better price," she responds. "It's already set as low as we can let it go."

"And how much is that?"

"Ten dollars a month. Well below the going rate. It's the best deal you'll find in Portland."

"Well, I guess I'm lucky, then." Pietro knows he won't find better in Portland, either in an apartment or a woman. "What's your name?" he asks.

"Helen," she says, before adding, "Helen Hemila. And if you'll follow me to our office, I can help you fill out the contract."

It's in this moment Pietro knows that, yes, he'll follow her—to the office and to the ends of the Earth if he has to. Ancient Greek myths could never feel this fresh, this vibrant. Pietro doesn't even care that at ten dollars a month, he'll have only about three months until he's really destitute, assuming he can subsist on scraps of day-old bread from the bakery down the block from his office. Assuming the bakery is still open. So many businesses in Portland have closed. Pietro's office still doesn't have any commissions. But right now, commissions don't matter, because he's a man on a mission.

"Can I take you out on a date?" Pietro asks as soon as he signs the paperwork.

Helen squints. It's not the first time a man has asked her out while she's on the job, but at least this man had the patience to wait until after their business was completed. This Helen is not of Troy. She will not be whisked away. She can take care of herself, and she is. She's the best salesperson at this property management company. She knows the city like the back of her hand. And she should. She grew up in Portland. She's Helen of Portland, and she makes the decisions when it comes to her love life.

"I'll go on one condition," Helen counters. "That you pay first and last month's rent. Right now. Just to make sure you won't skip town after our date. We usually require only one month at a time for this apartment, but I'm sure you can see why we'd want to take this precaution."

Pietro grins from ear to ear. He finds Helen's shrewd logic endearing. He can't help but imagine this sentiment is similar to what Claudius felt for Calpurnia after she revealed her shrewd logic to him.

The last time Pietro tried to make a condition, things didn't go as planned. But maybe this time, because Helen is the one to make it, perhaps things will go better.

Luckily for Pietro, their date goes well. Pietro and Helen fall in love right before Pietro's money runs out, and he moves in with her to save what he has left.

Somehow, the lease agreement for his apartment goes missing. The property management company is forced to let him skip out on the lease before it's up. Helen is usually such a stickler for filing contracts correctly. It's so odd that she would have misplaced it. But she's in love, and when you're in love, you'll do anything. Helen of Troy knows a thing or two about that.

Helen's apartment is much nicer than Pietro's could ever be, anyway. It's not much different from the unit she showed Pietro, but it's a wonder what this woman can do with a few pieces of art and some decoratively draped textiles. She's savvy and insightful, not just when placing people in apartments, but also when choosing the things to put in them as well. But did she make the wrong choice with Pietro? Is she just wasting her time?

Pietro's office still doesn't have any commissions, so it's the same as if he doesn't even have a job. And now Helen has invited him into her home. But she only did that because he was already in her heart. *Things will pick up*, she assures herself. She just needs to be supportive, and she is, both financially and emotionally.

Pietro likes to say she's so supportive, she's the Calpurnia to Pietro's Claudius, if they were characters in *I, Claudius*, but unlike Claudius and Calpurnia in the book, they're living off Helen's wages alone. Helen hasn't had time to read the novel to make sure it's a flattering comparison. And she'd rather not know if it isn't.

Pietro has a lot of time to read. Inspired by Helen's Finnish lineage, Pietro researches Scandinavian architecture, centering on the work of Gunnar Asplund, Willem Dudok, and Alvar Aalto.

With their work swirling in his head and love bursting out of his heart, he has a vision. He imagines himself marrying Helen. At the altar, they're surrounded by a beam of white light.

So, when someone approaches Pietro to design a chapel attached to a mortuary, he already knows what he's going to do.

His design features a pulpit bathed in sunshine from a circular skylight overhead, engulfing it in a beam of light, almost as if God were shining down from above with his love.

And God must be shining down on Helen and Pietro, and his career, because Pietro's design receives as much attention as Helen of Troy's ill-fated love once got her. Or at least as much attention as any northwest regional chapel design could.

It's not just the commission he needed to jumpstart his career and dig him out of this Depression; it's the commission Pietro needed to help him on another mission. The only thing, though, is deciding if it's worth the fight. He built his career at A. E. Doyle's firm, which still bears the man's name.

Is now the time for Pietro to place his name above the door?

Chapter Eighteen

THE FOUNTAINHEAD

First it was a chapel, then a housing development, then a shopping center, then another housing development, a theatre, a community center, more theatres, and more housing developments. An assembly line of facades passes over Pietro's desk. For some people, the 1940s are marked by war, but for Pietro, it's marked with work. He brings commission after commission into the office, but they are not big enough to allow him to take over the firm. He still needs that one project, that one landmark commission to cement his legacy.

Pietro hasn't been obsessed with his legacy only at work, though—he's taken it home with him. First one son, then another. Americans are sending their sons off to war, but Pietro's sons aren't old enough. Peter is two and Tony is an infant when the war is in its infancy, at least America's involvement in it.

As Peter gets older, Pietro allows the boy to join him at the office some days, as long as he stays out of the way.

Pietro enjoys spending time with Peter, but he doesn't have

much time at home, so if he's going to spend time with the boy, it has to be at work.

Pietro doesn't even have time to read Ayn Rand's novel *The Fountainhead* when it's published in 1943. But that's probably for the best. There's no need to read about Roark when you're busy being one. Perhaps it's like Helen's relationship with *I, Claudius*; she doesn't read it because she doesn't want to be disappointed. And Pietro doesn't want to disappoint his family, so he stays focused on acquiring projects. That way, one of these days, he can reel in a big enough project, one that will allow him to take over the firm. Maybe the new skyscraper he's designing will gain him some notoriety. He doesn't have a commission for one. With the war effort on, no one needs skyscrapers, but with none being built, *Architectural Forum* magazine is hungry for statement pieces to publish. So, the magazine asks Pietro for a favor.

"A favor!" Pietro shouts when an editor from the magazine contacts him to design a skyscraper in addition to all his other work. "Of course . . . I'd be happy to do it," Pietro continues, realizing the project could give him some clout.

But what will he design? What type of skyscraper will leap from the page into the imagination of some rich client?

"Vroom!" Peter runs around the room, playing with an aluminum airplane.

What type of material should Pietro use to make the building stand out?

"Nnneeaoowww!" Peter flies the airplane above Pietro's head, but it may just as well be a lightbulb.

"Hey, Peter. Would you like to go on a little trip with me?"

"Can we fly there?"

"We won't need to, but we can pretend."

"Vroom! Nnneeaoowww!" Peter flies his airplane out the window as Pietro drives them to the outskirts of town, to a factory that manufactures the aluminum sheets for airplane wings.

Portland has positioned itself as an integral cog in the war machine. Many businesses, such as this one, have sprung up to support the war effort.

"But when the war is over, what will you do?" Pietro asks the plant owner once they arrive. It's a question many a plant owner will ask themselves over the years to come.

Pietro tells the man about his design. And while it might only be a design for now, Pietro could use aluminum sheeting on the facade of a skyscraper with the surplus that will be available when the war is over. No one has ever done anything like that before, clad a skyscraper in aluminum. Too bad no one needs skyscrapers at the moment, only housing developments for the workers in the factories. And theatres and community centers to entertain them as well.

Pietro's mind wanders back to work on the return drive, to the same designs he's forced to do over and over again. But then Peter points out the window to a train as they pass a rail yard.

"Choo choo!"

"Choo choo," Pietro parrots before recognizing something about this train isn't like others he's seen. It's very dirty, but that's not what makes it different. What makes it different is how it's being cleaned.

Pietro pulls over and gets out of the car. He watches a man go window to window on the train, using . . . some sort of machine to clean each one. He's quick, not spending much time on each individual window. The machine is doing the real work, lightening his load.

If only you could use something like that on the outside of a building. That's the thing with skyscrapers, actually. Modern architects want to pack in as many windows as they can, but people don't enjoy cleaning them, especially if they have to risk falling, leaning outside a window however many stories up in the air. And how can you coordinate with everyone so they clean their windows at the same time, so the sheen on the building is uniform?

"Now, imagine if you use something like a painter's scaffolding and lower it down, off the side of a building," Pietro says as he scoops up his son in his arms to look at the man cleaning the train. "And then you send a man like that over the side to clean everyone's windows. Do you think people would like that?"

Peter nods. If he's learned anything playing in his father's office, it's that he should nod when asked questions like that.

Pietro sets Peter down. "Okay, it's time to get to work."

The aluminum sheeting—it would be a first. This process to clean the windows by having a man rappel down the side of a building—another first. And that's when Pietro tastes it, his thirst for firsts. With this cleaning innovation, he could design the building with windows that don't even open, another first.

And because all the windows would always be closed, the entire building could have air conditioning, yet another first.

These ideas build, one after another, until Pietro has designed a completely futuristic skyscraper. It's exactly the type of futuristic structure he told himself he wanted to create all those years ago when he met that Italian futurist Marinetti, and more recently when he designed a skyscraper for Cake. Too bad it's just a design. It'll just sit in a drawer, or on the pages of *Architectural Forum*, as a dream. It really would be a dream, wouldn't it, the possibility of breaking ground on something this groundbreaking?

His aluminum design would cement Pietro as a Roark. It would be the landmark project that would launch Pietro's career into the stratosphere. Then Pietro could pretend he's his own Claudius, the lead character in his own novel, a tale of his comeback and how great he and all his ideas are.

When Pietro finally takes time to skim *The Fountainhead*, he notes the two paths Ayn puts forward in the novel. You can be a Roark, a leader of men, making the world bend to your will. Or you can be a Peter, Roark's antithesis, eager to give the world what it wants and reap the rewards. One is to live a tortured life, suffering, but suffering no fools. And the other is to be a fool yourself, perhaps not even knowing the only reason for your success is because you're a sycophant to ancient styles instead of having a signature of your own.

That's not unlike the dilemma Pietro faced earlier in life, with Mozart and Salieri. One is the vaunted genius. The other is the vilified ingrate, not content to live in a world in which genius exists, and more than willing to help eradicate any evidence of his own mediocrity.

Which will Pietro ultimately become? Are those his only two options? A hot poker pierces Pietro's heart every time he thinks about his new skyscraper design. The resentment stirs up his soul, the type of resentment that can clog up the heart and leave it closed to embracing someone else's brilliance, even if their star shines brighter.

Then again, Pietro can't just worry about himself anymore. He has two sons. Which path will they take? One is already named Peter, but let's hope that is a coincidence and not a life sentence.

Chapter Nineteen

EQUITABLE BUILDING

Tony draws on the floor in his father's office, but he doesn't use crayons; he uses colored pencils. Tony loves colored pencils, how you can use the tip for a fine line or use the side for shading. One tool with two completely different uses. And once the tip gets dull, you can just use any of the sharpeners in Daddy's office to sharpen them up again.

Tony mimics what the adults are doing on the tables above, drawing houses he'd like to build himself one day. But most of the adults don't use colored pencils in their drawings. Just black— black on white. Black and white. Those colors are opposite. Tony is five, about the age Peter stopped coming to their father's office, and Tony is learning all about colors in school.

Peter stopped coming to Daddy's office soon after he started school. It's the weekend now, though, and Peter could have come, but he complains about having to get up too early. Pietro leaves around four o'clock every morning to go to his office. And that's exactly what it is: *his* office.

Pietro moved the firm to a one-story, concrete industrial

building that was converted from a garage. It's a modern look for a modern company. The design for his skyscraper clad in aluminum sheeting is no longer just an idea, a schematic on the pages of *Architectural Forum* between ads for Gold Bond Gypsum Boards and Zurn Plumbing Drainage Products. Now it sits on the corner of Sixth Avenue and Washington Street in downtown Portland. Or at least it will once it's finished.

"It's funny," Pietro tells Tony. "Most people think an architect's job is done once he delivers the designs, but in most instances, that's when the real work begins."

Pietro's new skyscraper had its origins in the one he designed for Ralph Cake, but this time it will be different, Pietro reassures himself. This time Pietro has his cake, and he'll be able to eat it too.

Pietro knows he shouldn't get his hopes up. Something could always go wrong. But day by day, as the crew constructs his vision and the building gets taller and taller, Pietro can't help but feel hopeful, not only that it will actually be completed, but that it will enable him to engineer his future.

This building, this commission, allowed Pietro to take over his firm. No longer A. E. Doyle & Associates, the firm is now Pietro Belluschi, Architect. There's a big sign over the door that says "The Office of P. Belluschi, Architect."

It's in Goose Hollow, about a twenty-minute drive from the Belluschi home in the neighborhood of Aloha. *Aloha* has many meanings in Hawaiian, to greet and bid farewell, and to express love and affection. But to the Belluschis, *aloha* means *home*.

Tony loves his family's home. He loves the quince cherry trees near the driveway, and the apple, pear, and filbert trees in the back. It's six acres of pure bliss, with a creek running through it. A creek where he can catch crayfish.

It's all the room a boy could need to run around. More than enough, really. Maybe that's why they have so many animals. There's Sweet Sally, the sweet donkey. Don Giovanni, the striped cat, who got his name because he liked to screech as loud as an operatic voice Peter and Tony heard on the radio. There's a black poodle named Frank and a German Shepherd pup named Tank, named after his mother, who was a soldier in the Second World War.

Scurrying around the six acres are six animals, including Peter and Tony, for Helen to keep track of. Despite the constant activity, life in Aloha can be isolating for Helen, so Pietro does his best to make it more comfortable for her. They say *aloha* to the interior wall near the kitchen, tearing it out, opening up the space to create an L-shaped living and dining space, making it so anyone cooking can still be part of the conversation. And that conversation is cozy next to the two-sided fireplace with a smooth concrete-sculpted hood.

If they don't want to dine indoors, there is the covered loggia outside. Pietro also covers the walkway between the house and a two-room shed, one room for wood and another for fruit, and lays concrete in between.

It's a seamless transition between indoor and outdoor space, something desirable unless you're trying to teach two young boys when to use their indoor and outdoor voices. In that case, it would be helpful if the architecture didn't confuse them.

"Perhaps a few small touches here and there could be nice," Helen tells Pietro. "Just to make it more homey, don't you think?"

"Of course, dear," Pietro agrees, even though his mind is already focused on architectural upgrades instead of finishing touches.

Helen adds rugs, décor, and Finnish fabric galore, making the house look like a Scandinavian store. Pietro spruces up the place by installing unpainted spruce on the walls and ceilings, further blurring the line between indoor and outdoor space. He also positions new windows to frame the trees outside, almost as if they were paintings on the wall. And Pietro doesn't just stick to the original farmhouse's floor plan; he extends it. As much as the boys were fond of sleeping in a pantry that had been converted into their bedroom, they enjoy their own rooms and second bathroom in the new wing even more.

After the renovations are done, though, Pietro is rarely home. In that way, the upgrades are just like one of his construction sites. Pietro is key in making it, but then he lets other people manage the maintenance.

And even when he is home, he might as well be at work. Pietro extended part of the living room to make a study. Helen, Peter, and Tony like to joke that you need to make a stew if you want to get Father out of his study, where he stews. It was one benefit of the L-shaped kitchen and living space: the aroma from the kitchen wafts over to his study, sending up the signal that it's time to emerge from his man cave and eat.

But Pietro doesn't always leave sites to their own devices once he's set sight on another project. And he doesn't always leave his children to their own devices either. Or at least he doesn't leave Tony. Tony still comes to his office. And Tony still rides shotgun in Pietro's Chrysler as he goes from site to site, checking on the progress of all the new construction sites and occasionally, projects from the past. What little boy doesn't love a construction site? The noises, the smell—it's swell.

Tony thinks Daddy's Chrysler is much more comfortable than his old LaSalle. Daddy had upgraded after he was in an accident. He never comes home before eight o'clock, but one night around midnight Mommy became concerned, especially with all the fog. Then she saw Pietro drive up in a new car. A train had hit Daddy's LaSalle, cutting the car in two. Luckily, Pietro only got a little boo-boo. He lost a thumbnail, but gained a Chrysler.

Tony was home that night, sleeping soundly in his bed. But he's in the front seat today as they head to a project Pietro is particularly proud of.

"The Equitable Building," Pietro says as they pull up to the gleaming aluminum facade of the future.

Pietro has to meet a contractor installing pipes on the upper floors, but before he heads up into the heavens, he spreads the floor plans on the hood of his car. "You haven't seen anything like it, have you?" Pietro asks Tony before continuing. "No one has. It's the first truly modern office building. The Equitable Building—doesn't that sound like a wonderful name? Better yet, a beautiful concept?"

Tony nods, parroting, "Equitable Building." Then he wonders, "What does that mean?"

"It means building fair, impartially, equitably, for all mankind," Pietro explains.

A LaSalle pulls up beside them. It looks uncannily like the car from Pietro's past. A ghost from his train wreck coming to haunt him. But this ghost isn't haunting Pietro over the train wreck of a car; it's here for a much deeper scar.

A man pops out of the LaSalle and says, "I need you to pop over to the Stock Expo as soon as you can."

"What's going on?" Pietro asks.

The man shrugs. "You'll see when you get there."

Pietro gestures to the Equitable Building. "I need to see about some pipes, but then I'll head right over."

The man nods, gets in his car, and heads off.

"What do you think it's about, Daddy?" Tony asks.

"Probably just something small. Half the time this job is about giving people a personal touch, making them feel heard."

Pietro attends to his contractor in the Equitable Building, then he and Tony hop back in his Chrysler to head to the Stock Expo. On the way, they pass through a few blocks with boarded-up businesses. Tony hasn't motored through this part of town before.

"Where are we?" Tony asks.

"Japantown. Or at least it was," Pietro answers.

The wood used to board up the windows isn't as neatly installed as the spruce on the walls at home. But it's more skillfully constructed than the wood at the Stock Expo.

"What is this place?" Tony asks as Pietro leads him past rows and rows of dilapidated stalls.

"Just like the man said, it's a stock expo, somewhere they show all the livestock and animals that come to be sold. Or turned into stew."

Tony and Pietro share a quick laugh.

"I think it has some fancy name like the Pacific International Livestock Exposition," Pietro continues. "But when I was helping them out, I think they called it the Portland Assembly Center, sort of a . . . relocation center for the Japanese they sent out of town."

"They sent their animals here while they went out of town?" Tony asks.

"No. No, not quite," Pietro says, his brow furrowed.

American citizens of Japanese descent were detained at this makeshift facility before being forced into internment camps in Idaho and Wyoming, but Pietro isn't sure he can explain this to his son.

"This was a quick project, Pietro continues. "Japanese people were told to leave their homes so abruptly and we were asked to build something fast, so I'm not surprised there's an issue. As you can see, it's not in use now, so the issue is probably about how to tear it apart, make it ready for livestock again."

Tony's eyes scan the hastily constructed, thin wood walls with peeling tarpaper. It looks like a barn, with sunlight peeking through the slats. The Belluschis have six acres in Aloha. Here at the relocation center, there had been six people to a stall.

There are so many things Pietro wants to say to his son.

He wants to explain that he knows this relocation center was wrong. The internment camps are wrong. He wants to explain that he knows he's had it relatively easy for an immigrant. Yes, people have their hang-ups about Italians. He dealt with a slew of racism, but when he came to Portland, he got a job. Then he turned that job into his own business. He became a citizen. But first-generation Japanese immigrants can't do that. The United States doesn't allow them to become citizens. It's not until the second generation, the ones who are born here, like Tony, who can become "real" Americans, whatever that means. Oregon passed a law in 1923, a few years before Pietro arrived in Portland, stopping Japanese residents who weren't citizens from owning land, or building their own businesses. And it was only in 1926, a few years after Pietro arrived, that the state finally repealed the last laws banning Black people from even living in Oregon. And that doesn't even begin to describe all the other indecencies Black people face. Restaurants still put up window signs that say "We cater to white trade only." In fact, more signs started going up in the last few years, when Black people came to work in the factories, feeding the war machine and the American dream. The factories make so many things, like the aluminum sheets that now cover Pietro's Equitable Building.

Equitable building . . . Building equitably, fairly, for all people. Pietro wants to tell Tony it's a goal, not something you can achieve with one building, but through building an equitable society. Of course, Tony is five. He's still learning his colors, so it might be too difficult to explain race relations.

“Over here!” the man with the LaSalle screams across the stockyard.

“I’ll just be a minute,” Pietro tells Tony. “I’ll be back as soon as I figure out what needs fixing.”

Chapter Twenty

THE GLASS HOUSE

You can see it from the hill: the Equitable Building. It's the reason Pietro accepted the commission from psychiatrist Dr. Clint Burkes and his wife Genevieve to build their dream home. Pietro had built the office of the future. That's what the early reviews say. And now, this is his opportunity to build the home of the future. His Aloha farmhouse was a renovation, but now Pietro gets to build this house from scratch. Or at least he will, if Genevieve lets him.

Pietro enjoys working with women. He prides his office as having a collaborative spirit and the women he hires understand that principle more than the men. In that regard, Pietro was glad for the war boom.

He hired Ebba Wicks Brown, a licensed architect. And Jo Stubblebine, who knows her way around interior design almost as well as Helen. There's also Marjorie Wintermute, who trained in interior design but was hired for her skill on the drafting table, and Mary Alice Hutchins, a Stanford undergrad who got her graduate degree in architecture from the University of Oregon.

Mary has many talents, but is specifically talented with specifications. These women work well together, and help Pietro secure commissions like this one, and two larger commissions for Reed College after the war, including a $240,000 science building and a $150,000 women's dormitory.

Genevieve could work in Pietro's office, if she needed to work. She has the talent, if not the qualification. It's not a problem that she's always onsite while her house is being built; it's that she keeps making changes during construction.

Her first request is for the house to have a flat roof, similar to those Richard Neutra is building in Los Angeles. The only thing is that a flat roof doesn't work well when it rains, which in Portland is nearly all the time.

"No problem," Pietro says after some consideration. Normally, an architect might push back at such an odd request, but Pietro loves solving problems. "I'll just have a drainpipe in the center of the ceiling," Pietro explains. "I can put it behind the wall, the one that runs through the middle of the room."

But halfway through construction, Genevieve comes to Pietro with a slight adjustment to the plan. "I want to knock out that wall so it's more open. There won't be any problems with that, will there?"

Pietro knows what Roark would do. Or rather, what he wouldn't do. Roark wouldn't have taken the job in the first place. Roark loathes working with clients. To him, the only reason a client exists is to commission his vision. But Roark doesn't have a family to feed. So Pietro is left with a conundrum: How can he keep the flat roof but still let it drain? How can he hide a pipe that is going to run right through the middle of the room?

That's when he has an idea. Maybe this architectural problem doesn't have an architectural solution. Now, upon first reading that, Pietro's idea might seem like more of a defeat, but Pietro isn't willing to admit defeat, and he's seen firsthand how you can achieve some solutions with a sleight of hand. Helen can often fix a design problem by adding a well-placed rug or tapestry. Jo and Marjorie studied interior design too, but have transferred their skills to architecture. Maybe the same could work in reverse? Perhaps the way to hide the pipe is not to hide it at all, but make it a feature. What would Jo and Marjorie do? What would Helen do? What would her Finnish friends do? Alvar Aalto is a Finnish architect who might understand. He doesn't even consider himself an architect, but an artist, with architecture being part of the same tree from which painting and sculpture sprout.

Twine. Pietro has seen Alvar use twine somewhere. Perhaps it could work here. But what could he do with it? Maybe just wrap the pipe in twine? It's a playful suggestion that turns into a practical one.

Pietro wraps the drainpipe with twine. And the hard edge of the pipe disappears. It becomes fuzzy, almost cozy. Now the pipe gives off the illusion of a ship's mast, especially since the room features a view that stretches to the horizon. Ta-da. Pietro has turned an architectural cheat into a feat.

The house's other features include glass windows that go all the way to the ceiling, giving the room that view, the one that extends past the horizon to Mount Hood. The ceiling is seamless on both sides of the windows, featuring fir boards that continue out onto the soffit. Cork floors balance the fir ceiling, and there's a rotisserie off the kitchen, just in case the Burkes want to pretend they're at a medieval feast. The bedrooms feature woven wood, almost like a basket, that soundproof the room until it's quiet as a casket.

Outside, in the garden courtyard, there's a wall made of Mount Adams stone, which occupied the property before the house did, and Pietro excavates portions of the wall to build the fireplaces.

Over the course of construction, Pietro pays attention to the seamless, continuous transition of the indoor and outdoor space, from the garden courtyard terrace to the one facing the city, so this house is homey regardless of whether it's sunny or overcast. But in Portland, it's mainly overcast. People say Hollywood shoots its pictures in Los Angeles because that city has so many days of sun, but Pietro knows some photographers prefer the overcast days because then everything is evenly lit and they have more time to get the right shot.

Sometimes artistic creations need that extra bit of time to come to fruition. With Genevieve's intuition and Pietro's ambition, he's sure there will be a lot of photographers wanting to take pictures of this project. Once complete, the Equitable Building and the Burkes House will be a vision of the workplace and home of the future. People will want to work there and live here, achieving the ideal, beautiful, seamless work-life balance.

If only Pietro could build that work-life balance for himself. Sometimes it's easier to be nimble in your career than with those who are near and dear.

Pietro knows he should be grateful. His designs, his vision, his business—all are about to receive their due. But he should spend more time with his family. That's why he's doing all of this, isn't it? For his family? He's building his legacy for them. Isn't he?

All this stress makes Pietro feel like a mess. His heart burns, not just with the desire to improve his family's quality of life, but from the stomach fluid that creeps into his esophagus when he hasn't eaten. Sometimes eating calms his heartburn, but sometimes it exacerbates it. Pietro becomes bloated and nauseous. Then he throws up what he's eaten and has to start the cycle over again.

He is losing weight, which is odd, because he has the whole world on his shoulders. Pietro is losing sleep, but when he lies down, his anxiety won't let him get a peep.

Like his father, Pietro has ulcers. But unlike his father, he doesn't want to tell anyone about it. If he told Helen, she'd just want him to slow down. But what can he do? Stop? He can't stop now. His career is taking off.

No one ever made it to the top if they did what Pietro should do and stop. Just because he feels sick doesn't mean he should quit. If only he could make the slight adjustments he needs to make, like with Genevieve and the wall, then maybe he could have it all.

Whatever the solution is, there's no time to stall.

Chapter Twenty-One

THE JUDICIOUS USE OF INTANGIBLES

A poetic experience is not unlike a religious one. You use words and texture to color the meaning of concepts. You focus on certain things in order to inflate the space they inhabit in the reader's mind. You use it to connect people and give them deeper meaning.

The only things that calm Pietro's ulcers are poetry and two Oregon church projects, the Zion Lutheran Church in Portland and the First Presbyterian Church in Cottage Grove.

Designing a church, like any building, is all about the judicious use of intangibles: space, light, texture, and color.

"In sensitive and skilled hands, space creates suspense and drama," Pietro tells the parishioners in both congregations. "The light a space receives, with its accents and shadows, hints at a mystery and becomes a means to deepen space itself . . ."

Pietro could have been a preacher. Or a poet, because he continues: "While texture and color may provide a moving poetic experience." But Pietro isn't a poet who works with words.

He's a poet who works with things that are even more ephemeral, even more intangible.

The entire purpose of designing a church is to make a congregation appear cohesive, connected. It's not about designing a place for them to sit down, even though churches in North America decided to upend tradition and provide a pew for every parishioner, unlike the churches in Pietro's youth. It's about designing a unified space, where everyone can forget their individual worries and unite as one, like they're all on the same journey together, like they're all in the same boat.

So, when he designs Zion Lutheran Church in Portland, that's exactly what he draws: a boat. Pietro gives the congregation an experiential embodiment of their emotional journey together. They're all in the same boat, so Pietro makes the interior appear like the inverted center of a ship, almost like all the congregants are in an upside-down version of Noah's ark. Why inverted? Partly for practical reasons. If it were a literal ship, there'd be no roof over their heads—but when inverted, the hull protects them from the sun. What would hold them together in water gives them shelter on land.

"A man on land is just as good as a drop of water on sand," Reverend Dan Hues, the pastor at Zion Lutheran Church, likes to say. "The desert will eat you up unless you gather enough drops for an oasis."

At First Presbyterian Church in Cottage Grove, Reverend D. Hugh Peniston's favorite line is, "Tell the Lord what you ask, and he'll say, 'Lordy, that's no easy task.'" Hugh likes to deliver that line before delving into his message. "God helps those who help themselves."

Now, Hugh knows that aphorism isn't in the scripture, but that doesn't mean it's not true. Hugh is fresh out of Princeton and the Union Seminary in New York. Now, he's tasked with building a new church for his first congregation. God has already gotten him this far, and it's his turn to take it the rest of the way.

Normally, that wouldn't be cause for concern—Hugh is a competent young man with a relatively good head on his shoulders—but there is something special about the lot he's supposed to build this church on that Hugh can't wrap his mind around.

The building site is on a corner lot with honey locust trees. No problem. They'll just cut them down and plant some new ones. Except the person who donated the plot emphatically wrote in the contract that the trees must stay untouched. That would be all right if all the trees were in the grove near the back of the property, but one tree stands defiantly dead center in the lot, right where they'd like to build.

Luckily, the architect they found revels in working around a challenge. Pietro sees the tree not as an obstacle, but as an opportunity to design a church embracing the full glory of the creator and the creations he placed on this plot before they decided to plop a church there.

Instead of just building around the tree, Pietro *designs* the church around it—an important distinction. He constructs a large, clear plate-glass window between the nave and the courtyard so the parishioners can pause and reflect on the tree from their pews between bouts of praying.

But while Pietro loves a challenge, some parishioners at First Presbyterian Church can be particularly, well, challenging.

"I don't see what any of this has to do with God."

"Why not just build a Gothic church? What's wrong with that?"

"Are you as naïve as our new priest?"

It's funny how the people who've attended church the longest can often be the least humble. The oldest and loudest congregants of First Presbyterian are adamant that the church have a classical, Gothic style. But both Hugh and Pietro want the church to have a more modern design, if for any reason, because, "Frankly, we don't have the budget to build a Gothic-style church," Hugh explains to them.

But it's Pietro who convinces them. Even though they can't afford a Gothic-style church, which Pietro thanks the heavens for, he's more than willing to take their ideas into consideration. Pietro leads the congregation on a walking tour of the grove, taking in the land in the same way he always walks around woods in the Pacific Northwest, slowly and in awe.

On the walk, Pietro can't help but talk, pontificating to the congregation. "This truly is a blessing, you know. I could never design a building as beautiful as these trees. I could never design something better than that which God has bestowed on us, but I will try to heed his call and come as close as I can."

Mary, a stout woman whose conviction for a classically designed church has been almost as great as her conviction for

Christ, approaches Pietro. "You're not one of those city architects, are you?"

It's not a question, but more of an observation. Cottage Grove is a cottage community, twenty miles south of Eugene. It's the type of place you move to when you don't want someone telling you what to do. That said, most of the people in Cottage Grove grew up here. And they rarely move away, so the residents' roots run deep, almost as deep as the honey locust trees.

"But I saw your design," Mary continues. "I don't know which way the sun rises in Portland, but here, it's in the east. And we have most of our services in the morning. So, if you're going to have this big window next to the pews, maybe you should have us facing west, so we don't get the sun in our eyes."

Pietro shakes his head. How had he not thought of that? "'And the Church must be forever building, and always decaying, and always being restored,'" Pietro responds.

"Is that from the scriptures?" Mary squints.

"Something close," Pietro posits. "It's T. S. Eliot." One of Pietro's favorite poets. "And speaking of a man who's divinely inspired, perhaps I just had a bit of my own."

Pietro walks right up to a honey locust tree and runs his hand across its bark. "What if I stained the wood on the exterior of the church . . . to match this bark?"

Pietro turns around to find Mary almost as sunny as the light she wants to keep out of her eyes. "I think that'll do just fine," Mary replies.

Pietro stains the outside of the church to match the honey locust's dark bark, but light wood and light color walls dominate the interior, except for one wall. Above and to the left of the plate-glass window that looks out onto the tree, a grid of colored glass alternates back and forth between violet and yellow. The colors mix, blend, and crash together, but produce something quite mellow, serene. As the morning sun strikes the window, it creates an interplay of violet and yellow that colors the other walls in its resplendence. The colors dance across the room as the day goes on, creating a light show behind the pulpit. It's a colorful display in a modern, contemporary church—almost the antithesis of what the parishioners originally wanted.

Even so, at the opening, Mary wanders over to Pietro and touches his arm. "I was fond of the old church, but I feel like I'm closer to God in this new one."

It's the greatest compliment Pietro could have received. And that's when he realizes: When was the last time his ulcers acted up?

Designing churches isn't easy. Actually, the stakes are much higher than in other structures. Design an office incorrectly and a man might lose his business. But design his church incorrectly and a man might lose his soul.

What is Pietro's goal in all of this? To build a legacy? To gain recognition? To rid himself of ulcers so he can enjoy some of that recognition? If so, even though the stakes are higher, designing churches doesn't fill him with the same anxiety as other structures. Instead of emptying his creative cup, they fill it up.

This could be his new calling.

Chapter Twenty-Two

WRIGHT A WRONG

Just because God is calling doesn't mean you have to answer. But Pietro does take the call when it's the American Institute of Architects, congratulating him on his advancement to Fellow.

"You should be proud of this honor," the AIA president tells him over the phone. And Pietro is. He is no longer merely a fellow within this fellowship, another architect in the bunch, but a Fellow with a capital F. The distinction gives him an enhanced importance within the organization. He has achieved the society's highest honor—besides the Gold Medal, that is. While there may be a dozen or more Fellows recognized at once, only one Gold Medal is handed out at a time. It's an honor so rare that the AIA doesn't even do it every year. In the past ten years, the organization has awarded the Gold Medal only three times.

When Pietro gets a copy of the Fellows directory, he pours over the names of the others in his esteemed company. He's one of three West Coast architects to achieve the distinction this year. There's Gardner A. Dailey in San Francisco and Hart Wood in

Honolulu. So, really, there are only two West Coast architects. Almost all the other Fellows live east of the Mississippi.

Pietro scans the names from previous years and sees that Richard Neutra in Los Angeles was made a Fellow the year before. There were a few more West Coast Fellows last year, but as Pietro goes year by year through the directory, he sees a familiar pattern. Most of the Fellows are part of the East Coast Elite, those rarefied architects who like to build high into the air, up where they keep their noses.

Pietro searches for names he knows: Ralph Thomas Walker; Henry Bacon; Louis Henry Sullivan, the father of skyscrapers. But Pietro doesn't see one name he expects, a man mentored by Louis Henry Sullivan who, in turn, mentored Pietro.

No, no, this has to be wrong. There is no Wright. How could Frank Lloyd Wright not be an AIA Fellow? He should have received a Gold Medal by now!

Pietro writes three letters to his fellow West Coast Fellows:

"This is an injustice of the highest order!"

"It's time to raise hell."

"We need to kick these old gents out of their comfortable seats."

Now, Pietro isn't quite a young gent. He's forty-eight, but in the architectural profession, he is still a relative whipper-snapper. Or at least that's how some people perceive him when they hear he wants to start trouble. But Pietro doesn't want to start trouble; he just wants to break the AIA out of its bubble. Why hasn't it recognized Frank Lloyd Wright for his brilliance? He's nearly eighty-one!

Wright has already completed a veritable cannon. There are houses all across America with his stamp on them, including the Hollyhock and Ennis Houses, which literally feature a concrete stamp Wright created, an integral part of their signature appeal. Then there is Pietro's favorite, Fallingwater, a house that cascades over a waterfall. It really is a wonder, warts and all.

Pietro doesn't even care that Fallingwater's bedrooms are so small, and the adjoining patios so large and numerous, that the cohesion between indoor and outdoor living is a bit humorous. The various patios promote seclusion rather than interaction, almost as if the house's inhabitants are independent streams that run parallel to each other, rather than belonging to one brook, like the one the house perches over. Wright designed everything around the waterfall. It's not quite a house built to be lived in, as most of his other houses are, but it's still a work of art in its own right.

That's when Pietro realizes why the AIA hasn't lauded Wright. It's his houses. Unlike a lot of the other Gold Medal recipients, most of Wright's work up to now has been in residential architecture.

"But it's American architecture," Pietro pleads to Thomas Creighton, editor of *Progressive Architecture* magazine. Pietro plans to lead a rebellious group to storm the upcoming AIA convention and force a vote to give Wright a Gold Medal.

"I'd rather not meddle," Thomas responds, acting more conservative than the editor of *Progressive Architecture* should.

Now, you might think Pietro is only as rebellious as someone who designs churches can be, but that means you're probably more familiar with the New Testament, whereas Pietro is Catholic. So, he's well-versed in God's wrath in the Old.

By the time Pietro walks into the annual convention in Salt Lake City, he has indoctrinated a small group of followers with his Old Testament and Italian futurist ideals. "I think it's a mistake to sit in the corner and sulk," Pietro preaches to them. "We need to pound the pavement. Now, we won't walk up and down the hallways with a megaphone, but we can be very articulate in our demands."

Pietro turns to a younger AIA member, Carl Koch, one of Pietro's new recruits, and tells him, "I hope when you get old and respectable, a new crop of young squirts will tell you to hurry up and move over."

Carl swallows. "Hopefully, I'll get in a few good years before it's my time to go." Carl is only thirty-six, but he studied at Harvard, first at the College and then at the Graduate School of Design. So, Carl's shot of achieving success is close to set in stone, especially because he was educated on the East Coast, unlike most of the "West Coast Radicals," as they're now calling Pietro's band of believers. But soon, Pietro's geography won't matter as much as his ideology.

"Frank Lloyd Wright is the best and bravest among us, near the best architect America can produce," Pietro says passionately to anyone within earshot. "If the AIA doesn't acknowledge his contributions, does it really mean anything if it recognizes any of ours?"

With this plea Pietro wins over William Wurster, who

hasn't become a Fellow yet, even though he's the dean of the MIT School of Architecture. It's the same school Ralph Thomas Walker, their principal opposition, attended before taking up an apprenticeship at an architectural firm, dropping out his last semester before graduating. Unlike Wurster, though, Walker became a Fellow in 1932, sixteen years ago. The East Coast Elites have trouble acknowledging someone's contributions unless they have a skyscraper in Manhattan. And Walker has two. There's the Barclay–Vesey Building, a thirty-two-story building that the elites say defines the skyline of Lower Manhattan. He offset the upper tower from its base, almost like a backdrop in the film *Metropolis*, a vision of Art Deco. Then there's the 1 Wall Street building, its street number signifying its rank, at least in Walker's mind, as the best building in the financial district. It's an asymmetrical tower with small concave swoops, all made of limestone. It's elegant in the way all Art Deco is, celebrating the luxury, glamour, and decadence of a decade that brought about its decline. Walker built both before the 1929 crash and hasn't had a big hit since.

"Why must we glorify the endless ribbons of plate glass?" Walker asks Pietro as he walks up to him, less of a conversation starter and more of an opening salvo, especially because he's referencing Pietro's Equitable Building.

"You suggest we just keep copying Art Deco all across America instead of trying to find something new?" Wurster retorts, standing up to Walker on Pietro's behalf.

Walker narrows his eyes, clearly stymied, turns on his heel, and walks away.

"I don't get why Wright likes him," Wurster confides in Pietro. "He calls Walker the only other honest architect in America."

"Maybe he's being sarcastic. Walker spent some time in the Camouflage Section in the Army, so I'm sure he knows how to hide his motives."

Wurster laughs and slaps Pietro on the back in the way well-heeled men on the East Coast do.

"Or maybe it's just his use of materials, or something like that," Pietro says with a shrug.

At the end of the convention, Pietro gathers 140 signatures from Fellows and other assorted members on a petition urging the AIA to award next year's Gold Medal to Frank Lloyd Wright.

"Order! Order! We must have order!" a sergeant-at-arms screams as Pietro, Wurster, and their rebellious group storm the convention floor during final deliberations.

"We demand a vote on our resolution! Or else there will be revolution!" Pietro shouts before the others join in, chanting, "Resolution or revolution! Resolution or revolution!"

"Fine. Fine!" the sergeant-at-arms decrees. "We will put it to a vote. All in favor of giving next year's Gold Medal to Frank Lloyd Wright, say 'Aye.'"

"Aye," a chorus of voices repeats, many more than the 140 who signed the petition.

"Votes against the resolution say 'Nay.'"

"Nay," a few voices bleat out. But only a few.

The resolution passes with overwhelming support. Pietro circles the room, shaking hands with everyone he can until his palms hurt. After Pietro laps the room, he realizes he's come full circle. Pietro has finally paid back the man who helped him get his start with the Portland Art Museum commission.

But Wurster doesn't want his campaign with Pietro to be over. "I'm going to run for AIA president next year," he reveals to Pietro. "Do you want to be my VP? Help shake things up even more?"

Pietro shakes Wurster's hand even though his palms hurt. He knows the road ahead will be hard. While Wurster made an ally in Pietro, he made an enemy in Walker. And they soon learn Walker will run against them.

"I bet he has a few tricks up his sleeve," Pietro says as they strategize how to win the next election.

But it turns out Walker doesn't have as many tricks up his sleeve, per se, as he does brothers in arms. As a member of the East Coast Elite, all Walker has to do is encourage attendance at the next convention amongst the conservative majority of the AIA, who live on the East Coast, for him to secure a resounding victory. The 1949 convention has the largest attendance of any AIA gathering on record and Walker wins in a landslide.

Even though they lose the election, Pietro and Wurster can't help but observe that they've won a greater victory. They witness Frank Lloyd Wright receive his Gold Medal. And the campaign has been good for Pietro's health. His ulcers haven't been acting up as much lately. Perhaps this is all he has to do to calm them, design churches and help his idols win awards. If so, maybe Pietro should pursue those passions instead of more lucrative projects.

Pietro wants to support men like Wright, but he also wants to be a Wright in his own right.

Chapter Twenty-Three

A LEADING MAN

Gary Cooper always plays the leading man. And he seems to have a habit of inhabiting roles that parallel Pietro's life. First it was Frederic in *A Farewell to Arms.* Although that story features an American ambulance driver instead of an Italian soldier, it still revolves around the heartbreak and heartache of war, something all too familiar to Pietro. The film was based on a novel by Ernest Hemingway. Pietro remembers the name—it's the same as the ambulance driver he met during the war. Apparently, Ernest had good reason to tell Pietro to remember it.

And now there's *The Fountainhead*, starring Gary Cooper as the indomitable Howard Roark. This one was also written by one of Pietro's acquaintances, Ayn Rand, who penned not only the novel but the screenplay as well. That makes sense because, as anyone who's become acquainted with Ayn can attest, she wouldn't give up control of the screenplay to anyone else.

As glad as he is for Ernest and Ayn's successes, Pietro feels a tinge of regret as he sits in the Paramount Theatre in Portland, watching Gary Cooper in *The Fountainhead* portray the leading man Pietro wishes he could be. Both Ernest and Ayn are leading figures in their field. Frank Lloyd Wright is one of the leading men of architecture. And Pietro is just a footnote in all their stories—a side character, not a lead.

The firm of architects who designed the Paramount Theatre also designed dozens of theatres just like it, indistinguishable from one another. This one opened as the Portland Publix Theatre before the name changed to the Paramount, but it easily could have been called the Denver Publix or the Phoenix Publix, because the architects simply dusted off the same designs they had sitting in a drawer. Every theatre features the same corny ornamentation. The same lackluster decor. The same Wurlitzer next to an elevator played by a man in the same white suit, playing the most ear-splitting organ music you can imagine. The organ music is so universally awful that Pietro can only imagine its purpose is to drive people out of the theatre and into the lobby, where they can buy refreshments.

In many ways, Pietro feels just like the Paramount Theatre: indistinguishable from others, and awful inside.

It doesn't help that the movie is awful too. Maybe Ayn should have had someone help her with the script. The dialogue is a disaster, but then again, the dilemmas are delicious. It's one of the weirdest romances Pietro has ever seen. How is he supposed to root for Roark's relationship with Dominique when she confesses to not having any emotions? She goes on a psychotic bender to manipulate Roark, so it does become satisfying to see her get her comeuppance. And then, when they meet again, now that Dominique knows the full breadth of Roark's talent—how wonderful is that moment? The look on her face when Dominique discovers Roark is not a side character in her story. She's one in his. It's a reaction Pietro wishes people had when they think about him. Dominique does have a considerable appetite for architecture, though. It's one of her saving graces.

One of Helen's many saving graces is that she likes to take Pietro out on the town, trying to get him out of his own mind. And the movie house is usually the perfect place to do that, helping Pietro escape into the stories on the screen. But maybe it's not the best getaway today because the storyline is too close to Pietro's own.

As he watches the movie unfold, Pietro detects this bubbling inside, this yearning that used to be a burning, something quite different from the ulcers churning.

"The issue which you are to decide is the crucial issue of our age," the state's prosecutor states in the courtroom scene at the end of the film. "Has man any right to exist if he refuses to serve society?"

It's an odd question coming from a prosecutor. Now, Pietro isn't a lawyer or a writer, but that doesn't mean he can't offer a critique of the two professions. Laypeople often critique his designs despite being ignorant of architectural demands. Pietro admits that perhaps sometimes it's a writer's prerogative to stray from reality in order to make a philosophical point. But shouldn't the state's prosecutor be asking, "The issue which you're deciding today is whether Howard Roark blew up the Cortlandt housing project?" If that were so, it wouldn't be a question, because Roark admitted to dynamiting the project.

Pietro knows another case in which the defendant completely upended the court's proceedings and made his trial about something other than the crime at hand. A year after Pietro arrived in the United States, in 1924, a man in Germany led an unsuccessful coup against the government. Similar to Roark, that man freely confessed to his crimes, but flipped the trial on its head, making it into a spectacle about lofty ideals instead. He used it as a platform for his ideology, launching his career, culminating with his eventual rise to power ten years later. That man was Adolf Hitler. And now Pietro sees in Roark's closing speech that Roark has been able to flip this trial in a similar manner. He's changing not only the rules of how trials work, but the unwritten rules of architecture and how architects view themselves. Whether that's for better or worse is still to be decided, but maybe Pietro could sway that decision.

"This is going to change everything," Pietro whispers to Helen during Roark's speech.

But she's so engrossed in Roark's rhetoric, she barely notices Pietro saying anything. "What?" she asks.

"Never mind," Pietro answers. He'll tell her what he said after the movie. And he'll tell her what he decided during the movie too. Because in that moment when Pietro sees Roark altering the definition of what it means to be an architect, Pietro sees how he's going to change things as well.

Pietro can see how influential this movie will be. Yes, the book came out six years ago, but if there is one thing young people like more than books, it's movies. Soon enough, there will be a legion of hopeful young Roarks entering the field. If architecture is a game of chess, then the game is about to become a lot more complicated. There will be many more pieces on the board as more hopefuls enter the field. So, how can Pietro stay ahead of the game? And how can he keep doing things that calm his ulcers instead of inflaming them?

The answer has been in front of Pietro the whole time. Or at least the entire time he's been watching the movie. Because before he and Helen paraded down to the Paramount, Pietro received a game-changing call from William Wurster. Wurster told Pietro he is going to step down as dean of the MIT School of Architecture.

"I don't know whether to congratulate or console you," Pietro said.

"Congratulations are in order," Wurster answered, "especially because I'd like to congratulate you, if you'd be willing to succeed me. Would you like the job?"

It's a question Pietro has been considering the entire movie. In one way, the offer was laudable. He'd be the dean of a prestigious school of architecture on the East Coast, giving him access to clients the East Coast Elite covet. But in another way, it was laughable. Pietro's salary would be 10 percent of his current earnings at his architectural firm, going from roughly $150,000 a year down to $15,000.

As Pietro watches the movie on the screen, he can see the writing on the wall. Architecture is at an inflection point. But is it a pitfall or a precipice of a new renaissance? The answer won't be up to him, but to the next generation of architects, the ones he can influence as dean at MIT.

Pietro doesn't want to give up architecture entirely. He wants to create *and* cultivate. Which brings us back to the moment when Pietro realizes, during Roark's closing speech at the end of the movie, how he's going to stay ahead of the game.

Pietro shuts the car door as a new world of possibilities opens up before him. "I'm going to start a revolution," he says. "I mean, I won't just be an architect, but a design consultant."

"That sounds like a step back," Helen responds.

Pietro shifts in his seat. "I can see how you might think that, at first, but it means I won't have to run an entire office. It's all so tedious. This way, I can be independent. Free. Not worrying about feeding families other than my own. Free to dedicate my time to my designs. And I can partner with other firms, as many as I like. Let them worry about their own staff. All I need is a secretary and a drafting technician. I'll give them my designs and they'll handle everything else."

"It sounds less stressful," Helen offers.

Pietro nods. "That's part of it."

It's true. That part of it will be nice. Hopefully, this move will calm Pietro's ulcers instead of inflame them. Beneath it all, Pietro knows he's making this move because of the other burning inside, the desire to be his own leading man. And with this, he could change the game of architecture, stay ahead of the curve by inventing a new strategy. Play a game no one else is playing, all the while guiding and mentoring the next generation that will decide whether his tactic is successful.

Simply put, it will make him the leading man of architecture. Or at least he hopes it will.

Chapter Twenty-Four

MASSACHUSETTS AVENUE

"In these dark times, we have a greater need of faith in the future than ever."

These are not merely the words Pietro says at the Reed College commencement right before he comes to Cambridge, but they're also the words he tells himself every day as he traverses the frigid New England terrain.

Pietro trudges down Traill Street and takes a left on Mt. Auburn. He trails that street all the way down past Harvard Square until it turns into Massachusetts Avenue, which he can then take to MIT. One road connects two universities, Harvard and MIT, and that's Massachusetts Avenue. But there's something that connects the two universities even more: their shared animosity toward one another. They are rival schools, always looking to one-up each other. Harvard is the oldest institution, but MIT had the first architecture school.

Pietro doesn't enjoy walking past Harvard Square. It's too busy. There are too many people talking. And Pietro has had enough of Harvard people talking—and MIT people, too, for that matter. Ever since Pietro became dean, he has endured rumors that he wasn't the first choice for dean at MIT. Apparently, the university wanted the esteemed Spanish architect Josep Lluís Sert for the job. Sert worked for architectural superstar Le Corbusier and calls artists such as Joan Miró and Pablo Picasso friends. Sert even had Picasso paint *Guernica* for his Spanish pavilion at the 1937 World's Fair in Paris.

How can Pietro assert himself as the leading man of architecture with men like Sert around?

The story goes that Sert turned down the job at MIT because his other friend Walter Gropius was already planning to step down. Gropius was dean of the Graduate School of Design at Harvard and Sert wanted his job instead. Gropius, the man passing on his baton, was well known for founding the acclaimed Bauhaus school in Germany. Bauhaus is not only a physical institution, though, but a philosophy. And Harvard could only get him to cross the Atlantic because of Hitler's rise and Gropius's Jewish wife. Before her, Gropius was married to the widow of Gustav Mahler, who was also one of the leading men of his generation.

In the eyes of some along Massachusetts Avenue, Pietro, the interloper from Portland, hardly has as much pedigree as Gropius's ex-wife.

Pietro had moved into a large house on Traill Street in West Cambridge, home to the Mount Auburn Cemetery, an overgrown, labyrinthine relic that draws a never-ending stream of students to its environs, ready to draw or paint or photograph its misery. Pietro found a house with a sizable living room and a conveniently laid-out kitchen, both things he thought he'd need to entertain in what was soon to be a never-ending stream of collegial colleagues. But people in Boston are as cold as the winters. Perhaps even more frigid.

And at first, there's no one at home to keep him warm. Helen didn't want to disturb the boys' development. They are ten and twelve. And Pietro took his new job in the middle of a school year. So, he's all alone.

The house Pietro occupies used to be part of the Elmwood estate, which was built in 1767 for Thomas Oliver, then the lieutenant governor of Massachusetts Bay, and his wife, Elizabeth. Everything in Boston has so much history. And everyone in Boston is so hostile to those without it. Even when the summer heats up and you think the citizens might thaw out, they retreat to their houses on Cape Cod to escape the impropriety of engaging with you.

Because Pietro must pass Harvard every day, he prefers walking along the Charles River, avoiding the Square altogether. He tries to keep pace with the rowers while he walks along the riverbank until he reaches Western Avenue. It takes longer than walking down Massachusetts Avenue, about two and a half miles in total, but it's worth it, and Pietro can make it in about forty minutes if he hurries.

Pietro is always trying to keep pace. President Truman recently appointed him to the Fine Arts Commission in Washington. And then he started working on the State Department Committee on Foreign Buildings. Besides Pietro's duties as dean, attending budget meetings and thesis committees, the State Department has him traveling to faraway places such as France, New Zealand, Australia, Korea, and China, consulting on problems abroad while running away from his problems at home.

Immediately upon her arrival, Helen knows she doesn't like Cambridge, or Boston either. Pietro hoped the change of scenery would stimulate her. He transferred all the work in his Portland office to the architectural firm Skidmore, Owings & Merrill, but he forgot to stop taking on new work.

His new strategy of working as a design consultant is going swimmingly, but because he's often flying off to exotic locales for his federal duties, it often means abandoning Helen with the boys in their new home.

Sometimes Helen thinks about what Pietro does on all his trips. And in these dark times, when Helen thinks, Helen drinks.

She's particularly sauced the night they have to attend a welcoming dinner for the incoming dean of the Graduate School of Design at Harvard, none other than Josep Lluís Sert.

The dinner was supposed to be held at the Harvard Faculty Club, a slightly underwhelming building when approached from Quincy Street. But when Pietro and Helen approach the door, a precocious undergrad informs them, "If you're here for Dean Sert's welcome dinner, it's been relocated to Alumni Hall."

Alumni Hall is only down the street from the Faculty Club, but it's worlds apart as far as accommodations. The Faculty Club is intimate, almost welcoming, whereas Alumni Hall is part of Memorial Hall, a High Victorian Gothic complex that includes Sanders Theatre. Memorial Hall was constructed after the Civil War to simultaneously honor the Union cause and how much money the North was printing after the war. Alumni Hall was built for formal occasions, but because everything at Harvard has the habit of turning into a formal occasion, it was quickly converted into a student dining hall.

Tonight, though, Alumni Hall fulfills its original purpose, all on account of Sert's celebrity status. A coterie of alumni brush past Pietro and Helen as they promenade through Alumni Hall's large, wooden doors. Many people on campus refer to it as the Great Hall, and as Pietro and Helen enter, they can see why.

"They must be able to hold half their students in here at once," Pietro says to Helen as they shuffle into the hustle and bustle of sycophants crowding into the hall, trying to hustle their way closer to Sert's inner circle. It's a cavernous room, rimmed with busts of prominent alumni.

It's hard to move. Pietro is nearly pushed into the bust of Daniel Chester French, the sculptor best known for creating the statue of Abraham Lincoln at his monument in Washington, DC. Unfortunately, it's the best interaction Pietro has all night.

"What do you teach?" someone asks Pietro before even asking his name.

"Architecture," Pietro responds.

"Ah, like Sert here. Isn't it grand we got him as our new dean?"

"Yes," someone else answers. "You know, it's men like him we need here. Men of a certain stature."

Pietro almost laughs as he spots the short Sert across the dining hall.

"Helps keep our students on their toes, if you ask me," the first man says.

"Not like they need much help with that these days. Perhaps it's because I'm in the philosophy department—you know how those students are—but so many of them, especially the freshmen, complain about feeling like imposters. Like they don't belong here."

"'Harvard: Where even our students don't think they belong here.' It could be our motto, next to '*Veritas*.' And that's the truth."

The two men guffaw with enough gusto for all three of them.

"Now, remind me," the first man asks Pietro again, "what subject do you teach?"

"He's the dean of the School of Architecture at MIT," Helen answers for him, sloshing the S in "school" almost as much as she sloshed liquor into her last drink before leaving.

"Oh," the two men say simultaneously, less taken aback by Helen's inebriation than by her revelation.

"I really must—"

"I should—"

The two men talk over one another before one says, "It was so lovely meeting you." Even though Pietro can see in his eyes it wasn't. At least the other man has the courtesy to swivel away, saying no more.

Pietro turns to Helen. "We needed to make an appearance and now we've made one. We're leaving once I congratulate Sert."

Pietro weaves his way through the crowd, cutting into the worshippers congregating around Sert, and sticks out his hand. "Congratulations," Pietro tells him. A quick handshake leads to a quick exit.

As Pietro and Helen walk home down the road that connects to Massachusetts Avenue, Helen complains to Pietro. "I thought this whole move meant you'd spend more time with our sons, not less."

"That won't be a problem any longer," Pietro explains. "I'm going to put both of them in boarding school."

Helen stops. "What are you talking about? Boarding school?"

"You're not familiar with the concept?" Pietro deadpans.

Helen double-takes. Under different circumstances, Pietro might be joking, but his pinched expression tells her he's not. She clenches her jaw. "It's going to tear our family apart. They don't need boarding school. They need *you*."

"They need to learn how to be independent. Life won't be easy on them, so we can't be either. They have to learn how to fight, to be the best."

Helen opens her mouth to argue, but she sees she won't be able to convince Pietro. At least not now. She knows he's been depressed, feeling second-best to Sert and all the other ten thousand men at Harvard.

Helen maintains firm eye contact. "Maybe we should move," she says. "Not back to Portland, but maybe Back Bay. Downtown. The walk would be shorter for you, just across the bridge, and you wouldn't have to pass . . . Well, the walk would be shorter, easier." Although she's drunk, it's quite a sober thing to say.

"In these dark times we have a greater need of faith in the future than ever." These are the words Pietro wants to say out loud, but he only recites them inside his skull.

He takes Helen's hand and marches her home, first to their house on Traill Street, then to a brownstone in Back Bay, just down Massachusetts Avenue and to the left, so he doesn't have to pass Harvard every day.

Chapter Twenty-Five

THE NARTHEX & THE KNAVE

Rejected. Dejected. It will never be erected.

One of Pietro's first jobs on the East Coast is to design a church and monastery for the Portsmouth Abbey School, a private Benedictine boys' school in rural Rhode Island.

Pietro is so proud when he hands over his initial proposal. His design is for a spare rectangular structure, but the roof . . . the roof! It would have so much flare. The eaves would flare out on either side and gently curve up in a slope up to the cupola. Then a thin spire would rise into the sky, holding up a cross for all to see.

But no one will ever see this design, except for Pietro, the fathers at Portsmouth, and maybe the editors at *Architectural Record* if he returns the magazine's call and gives the editors something to print. All because the fathers at Portsmouth rejected the design.

"It's lovely, but maybe something with more presence would serve us better."

"And maybe not a traditional, hierarchical, rectangular

church, but something more unifying, centralized . . . circular, maybe."

"We need an anchor. Something to center not only our complex, but our souls. Is that too much to ask?"

Pietro listens to the fathers' concerns closely. He wants to give them exactly what they want, but he's not sure what they want is him. Maybe it would be better if they hired another architect? Pietro would rather be an architect in demand than merely the architect on hand. Pietro only got the job because a young assistant professor at MIT hadn't designed the church to the fathers' liking, so they replaced him. Perhaps it's only a matter of time before they replace Pietro.

But until then, it is Pietro's job to lose and, well, if they don't want him, maybe he can bring artists they will like onto the project. Maybe Pietro could have them design a centerpiece or an altarpiece or an altar, something to astound or at least distract the fathers. Something to cement his place as the abbey's architect of choice.

The trouble is, the only artists who can consistently deliver profound pieces are often the most sought after. George Nakashima is one of the most sought-after artists on the East Coast and he only takes on clients who travel to his workshop in New Hope, Pennsylvania. Even then, he'll only accept your money if your interaction becomes more than a transaction. You'll only become his business associate if you become his friend first.

Eccentricity and talent often come hand in hand with artists.

In some ways, it's part of the myth, part of the story rich people tell their rich friends when they trot out one of George's pieces of furniture, or one of his sculptures. You can still consider something a sculpture if you sit on it, can't you?

Luckily, Pietro is positive he and George will become fast friends. Pietro will convince George to create an altar, maybe some altar furniture, a pew or two, any wooden masterpiece he'd be willing to make for a friend.

Pietro and George have a Pacific Northwest connection. George's parents live in Portland, and he was born in Spokane, got his degree from the University of Washington School of Architecture, then went on to MIT for his graduate degree. He attended the School of Architecture before Pietro became dean, so that's a connection Pietro can whittle into the conversation as well.

Pietro bobs up and down as he weaves in and out of traffic in a new Cadillac, the ultimate symbol of American success, hoping this trip will be one as well. He pulls up to George's studio, or rather, his *studios*. Two studios that couldn't be more distinct stand across from one another. The first looks more like a concrete block than a woodworking shop. The second seems more purposeful, but it's only half built on stilts. Even so, Pietro can make out the barn beams, the heavy oak frame, and the stone walls, both in and outside the shop. The second one sits on top of a small pond that could be an ode to Wright's Fallingwater, but is perhaps more aptly in line with traditional Japanese design.

"Welcome, Mr. Belluschi," George greets Pietro as he gets out of his Cadillac. "My new showroom isn't complete yet, so we'll meet in my current studio."

It may sound like an apology to some, but George's tone is even, as if he's merely pointing out a fact. George is a no-nonsense type of guy, wearing striped overalls covered in sawdust and a look of nonchalance that borders on indifference.

But Pietro responds as if it were an apology. "No worries. I'm sure we'll make good use of our surroundings."

George pauses, considering Pietro's words for a second. Then George smiles behind his moustache. He gestures and says, "Please, come inside. I'll make some tea."

Pietro wonders which of their many commonalities he should casually bring up as he wanders around George's studio. Bits and bobs of wood litter the space around the more substantial pieces of furniture.

A slab of wood, unfinished from a distance, becomes a coffee table as Pietro approaches. But it's not unfinished; it's distinctly done. The closer he gets, the more purposeful it seems. The organic grain of the wood thrives in its truest form, rather than being stunted into straight edges. And it's smooth and polished, not the work of some lumberjack, but of someone with a real knack—unlike the countless knockoffs Pietro saw littering roadside boutiques on the way up here.

"Here's your tea," George says as he extends a cup to Pietro.

"Thank you." Pietro takes a sip. "Tell me. First UW and then MIT, but both in architecture. Where'd you learn this craft?

From your parents in Portland? You know that's where I'm from. After Italy, of course."

George slowly sips his tea. "I learned it from a man in Idaho, Gentaro Hikigawa."

"Idaho? I didn't know there were any Japanese carpenters in Idaho."

George takes another sip. Pietro follows suit.

"We were staying there. Me, my parents, my wife, Marion, and our little girl, Mira. She was six weeks old when we arrived."

"Sounds like a lovely family vacation. Maybe I should take my boys. Where were you staying? Anywhere I should visit?"

"Camp Minidoka."

Pietro drops his cup, which shatters on the floor. "Oh, my God, I'm so sorry." Pietro hops to his feet. He needs something to help pick up the pieces. He searches for a dustpan, even though that will only be a temporary fix.

George sits stoically, taking in the scene. Being a master carpenter, George knows all about the modulus of rupture in woodworking. It's the measure of a specimen's strength. Every piece of wood has its breaking point, and every person does as well.

When Pietro finally finds a dustpan, he bends to sweep up the pieces of porcelain. He's about to place the broken bits in a garbage can when George stops him. "What are you doing?"

"I—I'm sorry. I'm cleaning up the mess."

"Who's to say it's a mess, that it should be discarded? Have you heard of wabi-sabi?"

Pietro has. It's the traditional Japanese concept of finding beauty, not despite but because of something's imperfections.

"You see," George continues, "I might make something beautiful out of this mess, given a little time and care."

George takes the dustpan out of Pietro's hands and sets it on his work desk before sitting back down.

But Pietro stays standing. His chin quivers. There's a lump in his throat that needs to get out. "I'm sorry."

"There's no need to be sorry."

"No, I—I designed the relocation center, the one you and your family must have stayed at before they sent you to Camp—before they sent you to the internment camp." Pietro swallows, but there's still a lump in it. "I'm so sorry."

"I know," George says before taking another slow sip of tea. "That's why I let you come here. Now, please, sit down."

Pietro does as George requests, and puts his head in his hands.

George leans forward. "I accepted your request to visit my studio because, well, I wanted to thank you."

"Why—why would you want to—"

George holds up his hand. "I'm speaking."

Pietro inhales, then sits back. He takes his head out of his hands and gives George the respect he deserves.

"They tasked us with making the barracks more hospitable, more like home, because we didn't know how long we'd be there. Hikigawa-sensei taught me . . . Well, he taught me what has become the reason you're here to see me today. I thought I had learned meditation in India, from Sri Aurobindo, but the way

Hikigawa-sensei interacted with the wood . . . He would meditate with it, and it would tell him what it wanted to be. It allowed him to create things that . . . exist. Things you can touch, but that are also beyond touch, beyond sight—something more like belief, on this deeper level."

George takes another slow sip. "But the most important thing he taught me is that every tree, every piece of wood, every . . . thing deserves a second chance."

George hands Pietro another teacup. "Please. Have more tea."

Pietro extends his arms, taking the cup with both hands.

"I received my second chance here in New Hope," George continues. "That's a lovely name, isn't it? And perhaps an even more lovely concept."

George stands up and starts roving around the shop. "My parents, Katsuharu and Suzu, returned to Portland. They returned to the community that spurned them. They said it was because they deserved a second chance—not my parents, but their friends, their church. They would quote from the catechism. Article three hundred forty-nine. I memorized it."

George shifts his stance. "I had time to memorize it. It says, 'The eighth day. But for us a new day has dawned: the day of Christ's Resurrection. The seventh day completes the first creation. The eighth day begins the new creation. Thus, the work of creation culminates in the greater work of redemption. The first creation finds its meaning and its summit in the new creation in Christ, the splendor of which surpasses that of the first creation.'"

Pietro looks down. He can't remember when he started crying, but it must have been some time ago. Maybe it was when he confessed about the relocation center. Maybe it was when George mentioned his parents. Pietro knows he was crying when George read from the Catholic catechism, a summation of the Catholic doctrine. He could taste the hot tears crawling down his cheek. And now, looking down, his tears create small craters in the sawdust, mixing with the spilled tea.

George walks up to Pietro and takes Pietro's head in his hands so he can look him in the eye. "Tell me. Are you in need of a second chance?"

Pietro's chest hitches. He wipes the tears from his eyes, but soon they fill up again. Maybe it's the tears or maybe it's George's selfless act of forgiveness, but Pietro swears he sees the face of God in George's. But God doesn't have the features of a man. He's more like a beam of light, a radiance, a shimmer. But it's not a glimmer. It's bright. And warm.

"Yes. Yes, I do," Pietro answers through tears.

George hugs Pietro. "Well, then, here. You have it."

Tea turned into tears. Now tears turn into beers. "I need a drink after this," George says. "How about you?"

Pietro agrees, so George returns quickly with two bottles. He sits down and takes a sip. "So, what do you need me to do, friend?"

Pietro will always remember this moment: The tang of the beer on his lips. The small sliver of foam on George's moustache. But mostly, he'll remember this sensation. And what he just saw.

Oh, how the world would change if more people could see what he saw. So, Pietro decides to recreate it.

George shined his favor on Pietro, and so apparently God did as well. Then, the Portsmouth fathers followed suit.

Pietro's new design for the abbey is a monument to the moment he had with George: The eighth day. The dawn of a new day. A day of redemption.

Pietro's new design for an octagonal sanctuary has a smaller, second octagonal dome above. He lines the dome with narrow slats of redwood interposed with stained glass that fills the nave in colored light. If you squint your eyes and know what you're looking for, you might think you're in a psychedelic Stock Expo.

George's altar sits below it, beside the altar furniture he also designed and the pews he made too.

George is a good friend to Pietro, and his work helps Pietro convince another artist to lend his hand to the project. Pietro had come across Richard Lippold's work in Cambridge. Walter Gropius had commissioned a sculpture of his outside the Harvard Graduate Center, and there Lippold's metal *World Tree* will forever bloom. When he saw it, Pietro wondered if Lippold might be interested in approaching something even more eternal. Lippold is an abstract artist, and what's more abstract than God?

Pietro shares his vision with Lippold, who responds by creating a centerpiece for Portsmouth Abbey Church. Lippold agrees to install a sculpture of fine wire filaments suspended over George's altar. The wires radiate outward into the nave, seeming less like wires and more like tiny streaks of light when illuminated by the stained-glass dome above. It's a piece that produces a transcendent, otherworldly sensation, almost as if the holy spirit, or God himself, hovers over you.

One of the best places to view Lippold's sculpture is from the narthex, the church's lobby, as you approach the nave. But Pietro prefers to pray on his knees, directly in front of it.

He already has George's, but it's here, where he feels closest to God, that Pietro prays for God's forgiveness.

Chapter Twenty-Six

THE CARPENTER

Jesus was a carpenter. And so is George. Perhaps Pietro can be one as well. Or maybe he can simply win the commission to design the Carpenter Center.

Harvard recently launched a new visual arts department. The philanthropist and pear magnate Alfred St. Vrain Carpenter, an alumnus, and his wife, Helen Bundy Carpenter, recently donated $1.5 million to construct a new center to house the department. The Carpenters' son, Harlow, recently graduated from the Graduate School of Design, which makes you wonder how much more they would have paid if their son could have been chosen to design the new building. But the word on the street and in the small academic circles Pietro orbits is that Sert is on the lookout for a celebrated international architect to take the project's reins.

Pietro knows he must win that commission. He has designed the workplace of the future, and the house of the future, so how about the school? But he's no fool. He knows Sert will sniff around Le Corbusier, his old workmate, for the project, trying to entice him to make the Carpenter Center his first building in North America. If Sert entertains anyone else's offer, it'll likely be just to make Le Corbusier jealous. Either way, Pietro knows he has to make his play.

"Josep! Josep!" Pietro flags down Sert on Harvard's grounds, laying the correct Catalan pronunciation of Sert's name on thick to emphasize their common European connection. "What a coincidence, running into you like this."

"Yes, lovely to see you," Sert says. "It's funny, though, how many coincidences I've been having after the news of the Carpenter Center commission came out."

"I think I heard a thing or two about that," Pietro says. "Actually, I was on a long walk and thought I might drop by the site. It's quite an interesting lot, as you know, sandwiched between the Fogg Art Museum and the Faculty Club, which more or less blend in with the rest of campus. But it might be a suitable spot to have something stand out. Visually, of course, because it will be for the visual arts."

Sert pauses before responding, "I couldn't agree more."

Pietro examines Sert's face and decides it's his time to strike. "I think you should consider an MIT architect for the project. It would send a good signal, don't you think? Our universities have more to offer each other than any petty rivalries between us. We all want the same things. I can draw up a list for you, if you like." Of course, Pietro will make sure his name is on it.

"Sure, give me your list," Sert responds. "Although I do have to warn you, right now my list only has one name, and I'm sure you can guess who that is."

"The French critic?"

"Precisely."

"You know Le Corbusier better than I do," Pietro says. "But do you really think you could get him to come here and do a site visit, much less oversee any part of the construction? I'd be surprised if he even came to the opening ceremony. Plus, what would he design, a grain elevator? You know he said that's the only American architecture he likes."

Sert purses his lips. "I don't know if you've heard, but there are plans to extend the campus on the other side of the building and the Faculty Club, past Prescott Street. And once I told Corbu about that, he pitched me on an idea to build a bridge between the two campuses, the old and the new, and to use this building . . . as that bridge."

Pietro can see it, the twinkle in Sert's eye when he talks about Le Corbusier's idea. He sees Sert's certainty. He'll do anything he can to help his friend get the commission. It's a sentiment as beautiful as it is frustrating.

Later in the day, when Tony accompanies Pietro over to a construction site, the twinkle in his eye is duller than Sert's, but it's still there. Tony is in high school now and he's been racking up win after win in painting competitions. He's spending the summer at his parents' house, away from boarding school.

Pietro and Tony approach a congested construction site

on the corner of Marlborough and Berkeley Street, only a few blocks away from their house in Back Bay. Tony wants to be an architect like his father, but he's smart enough not to tell him that, at least when Pietro is in a mood like this.

"One and a half million dollars," Pietro complains. "I'd have one and a half million dollars instead of a sixth of that, like I do with this church. And six more times the prestige. Not like I want to complain about designing churches."

The church in question today is the First Lutheran Church. When Pietro took the commission, he thought the $269,000 budget would be more than enough, but he quickly found that, between dealing with the swampy soil of the reclaimed Back Bay and higher construction costs, the budget would be as restricting as a corset.

"Worst of all, it's right here," Pietro continues.

"Close to home?" Tony asks.

"Exactly. A short walk from MIT, or heaven forbid, Harvard, where anyone—my professors, my students, my enemies—can come see what their dean is designing. A small church on a small lot in Back Bay. Well, hooray!"

"Just because it's small doesn't mean people won't care. Look at the Ronchamp Chapel."

Pietro inhales sharply. Obviously, Tony knows Le Corbusier recently completed the Ronchamp Chapel, but what Tony doesn't know is that Corbu is sure to get the Carpenter Center commission too.

Pietro exhales, releasing the tension in his chest and the desire to strangle his son. He looks around the construction site, taking in the boxy brick building. The south side of the nave has a couple glass cutouts to catch the sun, supplemented by a continuous crown of clear glass ringing the room, right on top of the walls below the ceiling. It's a simplified version of the sloped roof Pietro initially wanted for the Portsmouth Abbey.

"This place won't win any awards, but it's exactly what the congregation needs. Plus, I have to sit three hundred people in here and Corbu has maybe . . . What? Room for about fifty people, as far as I can see in the pictures." Pietro's face pinches. "He didn't design it for a congregation. He designed it for himself."

Tony squints. What can he do to cheer his father up? He's rather blue. And Tony still wants to tell his father about his desire to be an architect. Perhaps there's a way to combine the two. Either way, Tony knows he has to make his play.

"I want to be an architect, like you," Tony states. "Not Corbu."

Pietro considers his son's confession. "You know we're in a Lutheran church, don't you? You don't have to pretend I'm a priest and ask for my forgiveness."

Tony cocks his head. "I'm not asking for your forgiveness. I'm asking for your blessing."

"No. No, you don't want to be an architect," Pietro responds, straying a short distance away from his son. "You only want to cheer me up."

"If it cheered you up, it would only be a side effect and not the cause of my desire."

Pietro puts his hand to his chin and looks up at the ceiling.

"That sounds like a line from something. Where did it come from? Or is it just rehearsed?"

"I have been thinking about telling you this for a while," Tony responds. "But it's not something I wrote down."

"So you read it somewhere."

"Or I listened to my heart."

Pietro flares his eyes. "Sounds like you'd be a better poet than an architect."

"Well, I guess you won't know that for sure unless you give me a shot."

"You want me to give you your shot?"

"Someone gave you your shot, didn't they?"

Pietro smiles at his son for a moment, then his happiness wavers. The kid has passion, but passion can be fleeting. If Tony truly desires to become an architect, he'll keep pursuing it.

"No. I don't think I'll help you," Pietro says. "Plus, as you can see, there's nothing for you to do here." Pietro punctuates his sentence by turning away from his son to inspect something on the far side of the room.

"What if I designed the pews?" Tony asks. "I looked over your plans and I didn't see anything for them yet."

Pietro turns back. "Now, you may think the pews aren't important. But, my boy, they are. They need to be simple, but not simplistic. In their purest form, they fulfill a sense of utility, but more than that, they need to fulfill a sense of dignity. Not everyone can handle the responsibility."

Tony presses his lips together. He pauses, considering the

gauntlet his father has laid out for him. "I can," he says. "I can handle it."

Pietro pinches his face to stop it from smiling. "Fine. You can take a shot at designing the pews."

Pietro turns away again so he doesn't have to hold back his excitement, but his son stops him.

"How much can you pay?"

Pietro laughs. Tony blinks rapidly. What did he say that was so funny? Does this mean his father will take the job away from him?

But Pietro is laughing at his son's sheer audacity. It's one of the qualities Tony will need if he's going to be a successful architect. But when Pietro stops laughing, he spots the concern on his son's face. So, he stiffens up and gives him a stern answer.

"I can give you a dollar an hour."

Chapter Twenty-Seven

TO BE FRANK

Like father, like son. And sometimes the other way around.

Pietro is so impressed by his son's audacity, he thinks it's about time he got some of his own. Pietro rarely has a shortage of spirit, but the boy's bravado shakes something loose in him. A moment of rejection usually never lives only in the moment, but in all moments afterward. Part of the gnawing sensation says you're not good enough, that all the choices you've made until now aren't good enough. But, well, if life is a series of choices, then Pietro knows what his next one needs to be. He needs to try again. He needs to take another stab at winning the Carpenter Center commission.

Luckily, there's an event approaching where he can do just that. Under normal circumstances, Pietro would simply schedule a meeting with Sert. The man left the door open to receiving a list of candidates from Pietro, even though he made it clear such a task would be pointless. Sert already made up his mind. So Pietro must unmake it.

Some Harvard architecture professor is about to make

a presentation about a secret palace he's designing for Cuban dictator Fulgencio Batista. And the presentation is shrouded in as much secrecy as the palace itself. Pietro didn't even receive a formal invitation, only a word-of-mouth request to attend. Rather than keeping the event small, though, the secrecy surrounding these word-of-mouth presentations often has the effect of increasing attendance rather than limiting it. Professors bring their assorted protégés to mix and mingle, trying to decipher which students will have a successful career in architecture after their schooling. And the students hope this show of camaraderie will get them in on the ground floor, so to say. Pietro has one such student in mind, and that's I. M. Pei.

"He's so talented, he could start his own practice," Pietro says as he introduces Pei to Sert.

"Yes, that's what I've been hearing about him as well," Sert says, nodding toward the young man. "Although, remind me, I seem to remember hearing things about Mr. Pei before you took over as dean."

It's true. Pietro rubs the back of his neck. I. M. Pei isn't so much a student but an alumnus. And one who graduated from the MIT School of Architecture about a decade before Pietro became dean. And even though Pei is one of the school's most illustrious new alumni, Pietro thought he might slip him under Sert's radar.

Pei's owlish glasses make him stand out in the crowd, as if being born in China didn't already do enough of that for him, especially in this lily-white flock. Pei had recently become a

US citizen. His timeline of entry to citizenry was similar to Pietro's. So, perhaps that is why Pei steps forward to come to Pietro's rescue.

"I was delighted to receive Mr. Belluschi's invitation to join him," Pei says. "I hope I can glean some stories from him this evening. His Equitable Building . . . there's no weight to it. It has such a very fine . . . Belluschi touch to it. And that's how I know he's one of the greats."

Pietro clasps Pei's shoulder. "You're too kind."

Sert sets his jaw. "Very well. Let me introduce you to someone who might give you a run for your money one day, a young architect under my tutelage at this very moment . . . A current student, actually, Mr. Frank Gehry."

"It's a pleasure to meet you," Gehry says as he shakes Pietro and Pei's hands.

The lights flicker. "Time to take your seats, gentlemen," an announcer lets everyone know.

"I didn't know this was such a show," Pietro says. "Very theatrical."

"Do you know what the lecture will be about?" Gehry asks Pietro. "Dean Sert says he wanted it to be a surprise."

The lights flicker again.

"Well, I guess you're about to find out," Sert says, before starting to lead Gehry inside. Before he does, though, Pietro taps Sert on the shoulder. "I just need a moment."

"I'll be there in a minute," Sert says as he gestures for Gehry to find his seat.

Pietro takes Sert aside. "After the presentation, I was hoping I might give you another one of my own. Architect to architect. Brother to brother. I have some thoughts on the design for the Carpenter Center."

"I'm sorry," Sert responds. "I thought I told you. I've already given the project to Corbu."

Pietro's cheeks burn like he's been spurned.

"I'm sorry," Sert says again before he heads inside.

The lights flicker, but Pietro doesn't seem to notice.

"Shall we find our seats?" Pei asks from a short distance away.

Pietro nods, but there is only a glimmer of recognition in his eyes. His pupils dart around in their sockets. In that respect, they are like Pietro's mind. How could he be so stupid? So foolish? Sert had already made it clear Le Corbusier was his man, but Pietro pushed ahead anyway with his own plan. And now that his plan exploded in his face, Pietro simmers in the disgrace.

Pietro takes his seat next to Pei, but he can hardly pay attention to the presentation. What does the palace look like? Pietro can't quite tell. Or perhaps he just doesn't care. Most of the presentation doesn't emphasize the palace anyway, instead centering on the structures meant to secure it: the walls, the moats, the preventive measures against boats. All to protect one man, Fulgencio Batista. He was the president of Cuba, then relocated to Florida. Then he moved back to Cuba in the most spectacular fashion, or some might say an attack. He ran for president again, but instead of waiting for the democratic elections to finish, he staged a coup against the Cuban government with the backing of the United States, suspended the Constitution, and started killing all those who opposed him. If there were ever a man who needed to visit Pietro's Portsmouth Abbey, Batista is it.

Pietro understands his passion, the drive to show your opponents who's boss. But Pietro doesn't want to achieve his aims with any loss. Even thinking about doing something like that makes him cross.

Pietro can't. He can't sit here any longer. He can't listen to whatever presentation is being made about ways to make this dictator feel comfortable, in control. There are certain men who control more power than they should in this world and Pietro can't sit around while someone talks about a dictator, whether it be the one in Cuba or the one sitting across the room from him who gives all the important commissions to his friends without considering the contributions someone else could make. Pietro bolts to his feet, but exits as discreetly as he can.

Pei stays seated, not sure whether Pietro is leaving or if the old man's bladder demands some relief.

But there is one protégé who joins Pietro on his escape. Or perhaps it's Pietro who is joining him on his.

Frank Gehry is about ten paces ahead of Pietro, not taking a break from the presentation, but breaking free from it. Gehry's gait is brisk.

"Hey! You there!" Pietro calls.

Gehry turns on his heel, his face clenched as tightly as if it were a fist. But Gehry relaxes when he sees that Pietro is his pursuer. "Oh, it's—I thought—how are you, Mr. Belluschi?"

Pietro catches up to him. "Couldn't take any more of that either, could you?"

Gehry smiles, but it wavers. "No, not really."

Pietro nods. "Me either."

Gehry chuckles. "No, I don't suppose you could, could you? Surprised you came here at all, if I'm being honest, sir."

Pietro shifts his weight from one foot to another. "And why would you say that?"

Gehry looks back toward the auditorium, then plants his feet. "'In these dark times we have a greater need of faith in the future than ever. By the symptoms of current events our civilization may commit suicide on a tremendous scale, and in a shattering shortness of time.'"

Pietro cocks his head to the side.

"Those are your words, aren't they, sir?" Gehry asks. "It's been a while since I read your address to . . ."

"Reed College," Pietro offers.

"Yes, that's right. Once I read that address, I thought . . . well, to be frank, sir—"

"And you are," Pietro interjects.

"I'm sorry, sir?"

"Frank. You are . . . Frank."

Gehry lowers his head, shuts his eyes, then gives Pietro one short chortle. "I'm sorry."

"For what?"

"I didn't realize you were trying to make a joke."

"So, now that you realize I was, why aren't you laughing?"

"Because . . ." Gehry gestures vaguely toward Pietro. "I didn't think you'd . . ." His eyes scan back toward the auditorium. "And I didn't think that would be . . ."

"Yes?"

"It's all coming to me as a bit of a surprise, I guess. Not quite what I envisioned."

Pietro's posture perks up. "And what is that? What you envisioned, that is?"

"I thought everyone would be more socially engaged, like you. Not sitting around discussing how to design for dictators but, you know, how to make a real difference."

Pietro smirks. "But that doesn't explain why you didn't laugh. What do I have to do, slip on the ice or something?"

Gehry chuckles. "I'm sorry. I don't know if it's the cold, but people haven't quite been as cordial here in Cambridge as I expected them to be."

Pietro nods. "I know exactly what you mean."

"I don't know if I'm going to continue my studies here at Harvard, if I'm being honest."

Pietro places a hand on his chin. What advice should he give this young man? Pietro has always been keen to tell someone to follow their own path. But he doesn't want to be the one responsible for Sert losing one of his rising stars. Pietro wants to avoid that fight. Or at least the aftermath.

"Hmm," Pietro vocalizes, "I've always said, 'You're wasting your time if you're working for someone else.' And if this isn't working for you . . . then I think you know what to do."

"Yes, I . . ." Gehry opens his mouth, then sets his jaw, shakes Pietro's hand, and says, "Thank you, sir," before setting off.

As the darkness swallows Gehry in the night, Pietro sees something else. Something quite bright.

It's the hope that Pietro might find someone, or something, to set his course right.

Chapter Twenty-Eight

OR, THE WHALE

Pietro doesn't need to read *Moby Dick* to know it's about a man on the hunt for a large whale. He doesn't need to read it to realize he's on a similar journey as well. Or at least he was. Unlike Ahab, Pietro has already harpooned a whale and brought it to shore. But that doesn't mean he shouldn't try for a few more.

Pietro sits in St. Mark's Square in Venice, once a sailing and whaling capital of the world. He sips an espresso, soaking up the sun and his success as he waits for someone.

Pietro taps his foot, but he's not impatient. And he has nothing to worry about. Pietro is already on a panel of architects overseeing the largest arts complex in the United States, a whale otherwise known as Lincoln Center. The assembled all-star team reminds Pietro of the storied artists and artisans Ludovico Sforza gathered to create the new School of Athens in the Renaissance. Unfortunately, like Ahab, Ludovico's ambition outgrew his ability and he died striving for recognition.

Given Ludovico's group, then, that would make this Lincoln Center project the new, new School of Athens, so to say. The leading minds of the day working toward a common goal—let's just hope they have a happier end than Ludovico's lot.

Pietro's cohort includes a man he has long been a fan of: the Finnish architect Alvar Aalto. And there's the Swede Sven Markelius, along with the Austrian architect Walter Unruh, as well as Marcel Breuer, Henry Shepley, and Philip Johnson, who designed the recently completed Seagram Building with Mies van der Rohe. It's the only office tower built in the past ten years that has a shot at unseating Pietro's Equitable as the office building of the future.

Wallace Harrison is overseeing these architects. Although all the architects are divas, Harrison is the one who sings the loudest. He's the architect of choice for the Rockefeller family, having designed Rockefeller Center, which carries weight even though the Rockefeller's aren't the clients for this project.

Before Lincoln Center, the Carpenter Center would have been the perfect opportunity for Pietro to test his ability to design a school, but now, as the man he's meeting approaches, Pietro knows he's about to reel in a much shinier jewel.

William Schuman struts across St. Mark's Square as if he's walking to a score he composed himself, because he probably is. He's a balding composer turned president of Juilliard. And he's currently in a bind, but he doesn't seem to mind.

"*Buongiorno*," Schuman purrs he approaches Pietro. He spins around, taking in the air, the square, all without a care.

"*Buongiorno*, Mr. Schuman," Pietro says as he shakes his hand.

A waiter sets down an espresso.

"I hope you don't mind," Pietro continues, "but I told them to bring your espresso as soon as you arrived, so you wouldn't have to wait an instant."

"That's very considerate. Thank you," Schuman says as they sit, while sizing Pietro up. "You're always so considerate, aren't you?"

"I try my best," Pietro responds. "And thank you for meeting me here. That was very considerate of you."

"It's a pleasure. What a grand coincidence that we're here at the same time. Both sightseeing."

"Venice seems to suit you well," Pietro compliments.

"I have to say, it's almost like the city has me under its spell." Schuman laughs. "It's all been quite relaxing," he continues between sips, "especially given the tension of trying to find an architect for our new school. You have, of course, been more than considerate, being the man you are, but all six architects you recommended to us . . . none of them were quite right, if you don't mind my saying so."

Pietro puts his cup to his lips, but doesn't drink.

Schuman takes another sip. "That Pei fellow and what's his name? Ed?"

"Eduardo."

"Both men were quite impressive, but everyone . . ." Schuman adjusts his seat, leaning in as if he has a secret. "They all came in with their idea of what the school should look like, but I'm not sure any of them have captured the spirit of what we're trying to accomplish at Juilliard."

Pietro nods. He recommended a number of architects to

Schuman, including Eduardo Catalano, a young Argentine architect Pietro brought to MIT as a professor a few years back. Catalano's work with hyperbolic paraboloids impressed Pietro. But instead of being inspired by Catalano's paraboloids, Schuman ended up annoyed.

"You wouldn't be interested in taking a stab at it, would you?" Schuman asks. "You'd be doing me quite the favor."

A pulse of tension passes through Pietro's body, but he fights it. He tries to relax his muscles, but it takes a lot of energy to look this nonchalant. "I suppose I could give it a shot," Pietro says as he takes a sip.

"What do *you* think the school should look like?" Schuman asks.

Pietro pushes back. "How could I tell you what the building will look like unless I know how you'll use it?"

Schuman squints, sips. Pietro leans in.

"Some of these young architects, they look up to people like Frank Lloyd Wright. And I do too, but as brilliant as he is, he does things like . . . conceiving the form of the Johnson Wax laboratory before he even has a client. And then you're stuck with whatever he's given you, even if it has no relation to how you need it to function."

Pietro waves over to the waiter. "*Due espressi, per favore.*" The waiter nods. Pietro turns back to Schuman and gestures at his cup. "You finished that one, didn't you?"

Schuman looks down, nods. "How did you know?"

"Three sips," Pietro says. "That's how long it takes to drink an espresso—if you're drinking it like an Italian."

Schuman sits back, smiles. "When in Rome . . . er, Venice, I suppose."

"You see," Pietro continues, "it is possible to anticipate what people want, but architecture isn't the same as espresso. For a school—especially one with a reputation like Juilliard, which has not just a name but a legacy to live up to—I could only make my recommendations after listening to the people who will use the space. Who are they? What do they do? What do they want? It's a conversation, not a conclusion."

Schuman sits upright, his smile gone. But it's not because he's sullen. It's because despite what Pietro is saying, Schuman has reached his own conclusion. "Perhaps it's this city that has me under its spell. Or perhaps it's you."

Pietro laughs. "You're too kind."

The waiter sets down their espressos and Schuman holds his up for a toast. "Let's hope it's not a siren song."

They click cups and sip their drinks. Then Schuman sets his cup down and gets down to business. "So . . . who would you like to talk to first?"

"What do you play?"

"When are your classes?"

"How much time do you have between rehearsals?"

"How much do you practice?"

"That much?"

"When do you sleep?"

"I don't know how you do it all."

That last one isn't a question. But it is Pietro's honest

reaction to the schedule most students and teachers keep at Juilliard. These students wake up early in the morning, do their own warm-ups, sometimes for hours at a time, then hop around all day from class to class, from ensemble to ensemble, finding space for solo practice in between, all while trying to get enough shut-eye and normal human interaction not to go insane.

Luckily, Pietro has Eduardo Catalano to keep him from going insane. Catalano helps him balance all the demands of the students, teachers, administrators, donors, and other assorted individuals, all who want their say.

Even though Schuman soured on the six architects Pietro sent him, Pietro wanted to give a younger architect a shot, so he selected Catalano to join him on the project. Together, based on the testimonies they're collecting, the school they envision is closer to a beehive than a building. So, Pietro and Catalano design the school with that in mind, creating an intricate system of organically interconnected spaces. The rooms flow together like jazz, but are composed like classical music, each section harmonizing with the others.

It's an approach that wins over Schuman and the selection committee, and wins them the contract.

The third whale is not much of a tale, although it is perhaps the largest.

Many architects had been clamoring for the Pan Am Building, soon to be the largest office building in the world. The plan is to set it atop the iconic Grand Central Station. But should they design something to complement Grand Central

Station, or to compete with it? Whatever they design could be to the station's detriment.

The challenge inspires many architects, but perhaps none more so than I. M. Pei. Pei designs a spire using Catalano's advances in engineering. But rather than having the spire sit atop the building, the spire *is* the building itself. It's a conical structure cinched in at the waist, almost as if it were a woman. Perhaps that is why she's wearing a crown. Or perhaps that is the point Pei is trying to make. Rather than design something to sit atop Grand Central Station, he crowns it, giving the station the designation it truly deserves.

But sometimes structures don't get the recognition they deserve. Pei's doesn't. It's a magnificently futuristic spire, one that would have made Roark proud, and perhaps that's why the developers didn't go forward with Pei's vision—because his vision wasn't their own.

Pei was listening to the future. Pietro listens to developers; he had already won accolades with his approach to Juilliard due to his reputation to listening to his client's demands. So, the developers for the Pan Am Building were curious to see if Pietro would listen to a few of theirs. First item on the docket: There is a lot of work involved with a project like this, so would Pietro be willing to share the workload with Walter Gropius? Would he work with the man who used to be dean at the Harvard Graduate School of Design? The legendary founder of Bauhaus? Would he allow that man to come in and overshadow him?

Gropius has a lot more to gain out of this project than Pietro. Gropius has a storied career, but he lacks a major commission to etch him in stone as a major architect. Rather than being upset that the developers want to set him up with someone who could steal his thunder, Pietro looks forward to the meeting of the minds with Gropius. Who knows, it might be another School of Athens, similar to what he's doing over at Lincoln Center. Or perhaps Gropius can be Thor and have the thunder, and Pietro can find something else from some other god.

The larger the project, the more credit there is to go around. And it's only by sharing the credit that Pietro can do all three at once: Lincoln Center, Juilliard, and now the Pan Am Building. Three whales.

But Pietro is the one who feels harpooned.

Chapter Twenty-Nine

MARJORIE & MESSALINA

Having surgery for ulcers is a funny thing. The worse you worry about the surgery, the more you need it. Pietro is busier than ever, so his ulcers are busier than ever as well.

There's only one word to describe ulcers: hell. The fire burning inside him churns like brimstone. All that separates you and the underworld is a remarkably thin barrier, the lining of your digestive tract. And when that deteriorates, your entire world does as well.

Luckily, Pietro's surgery goes well, at least as well as emergency surgeries can. When Pietro wakes up, he can't detect pain in his abdomen, but then again, he can't feel much of anything.

Perhaps that's why he reacts so cooly when he finds out that his secretary quit.

"Oh, she did? Well, I'll need to do something about that, now, won't I?"

Apparently, similar to Pietro, she couldn't handle the pressure of working on so many projects at once. In an architectural office, the resignation of a secretary, however talented, isn't normally much of a blow. But because, as a design consultant, Pietro only keeps the overhead of a drafting technician and a secretary, Pietro has lost half his staff.

Pietro relies on the employees of his partner companies to do the lion's share of the work, which is a financially convenient arrangement for him, especially because Pietro only hires his drafting technician by the hour and MIT pays the salary for his secretary.

So, if Pietro is going to avoid a return trip to the surgical table but continue harpooning whales, he must keep his stress level to a minimum. That means he'll have to find someone smart, capable, and experienced to be his new secretary.

"I'll do it," Helen says eagerly.

And it's true, she really would like to be his secretary. She's had a hard time since their move to Boston. Helen grew up in Portland. All her friends and family are there. And ever since the boys were sent to boarding school, she's been all alone at home, especially because Pietro's job keeps him busy not only during the workday, but at all odd hours of the night as well.

Pietro pauses, considering whether she's actually serious. "No, you don't have to do that."

"Actually, I'd like to," Helen reiterates. "And I know what you're going to say, but it's not just so I can get out of the house."

"It's this work that pays for the house, you know."

"And that's precisely why I think I should be a part of it." Helen looks around. "All this." She steps forward, touching Pietro's chest. "We almost lost it because of your health scare. So, I think I should be there to help protect it. All of it."

Pietro palms his forehead. "If you're homesick, you're more than welcome to take a trip back to Portland."

Helen sets her hands down at her sides as if she's presenting herself formally. "Will I have enough vacation time to do that at my new job?"

"You don't have the job yet."

"Well," Helen says, folding her hands in front of her, "then I'd like to formally request an interview."

Pietro almost smiles. "Please leave your resume at my office. And we'll . . . I'll call you if we'd like to move forward with your candidacy."

"At your office? I'm your wife!"

"That's why I want you to drop it off at my office. If this were truly going to work, then we'd need to keep these two worlds separate. There would be our home life and our work life, or else both will suffer."

"Okay, then. I'll drop it off at your office."

"It's your funeral," Pietro dismisses.

"No!" Helen screams. "It was almost *your* funeral!" Her hands shake with anger. She takes a seat, shuts her eyes, and sits on her hands to stop them from trembling. "I think we could make it work if we truly wanted it to."

Pietro averts his eyes. "I think it's for the best. You're not very well qualified for the position."

Helen takes a deep breath and stands. "Well, we'll see about that, won't we?" She marches out of the room, her feet clacking across the wood floors.

Pietro stands there for a moment, wondering if she's going

to return, but then he hears the clacking of their typewriter in the other room. Helen must be working on her resume.

Many women have been working on their resumes. When Pietro returns to his office, he finds a stack of them. He placed the advertisement for his secretary's replacement in the newspaper while he recovered in the hospital, and it seems there are many candidates as eager to get back to work as he is.

Pietro sifts through the stack, then he hears a knock on the door. "Come in!" he calls.

Helen enters, plops her resume on top of the stack, then steps back. "Thank you for your consideration."

Pietro smiles as he scans the resume she put together. Helen is an impressive woman. She took care of him while he was getting his footing all those years ago. Perhaps now it's the time for him to return the favor.

Pietro sets her resume down next to the stack of others. But would it be fair to give her the position? Perhaps he should interview other candidates to make it look fair. His salary is already going to their household. Surely, it might look suspicious if his secretary's did as well.

"Do you speak Italian?"

"How's your shorthand?"

"What would you do if I asked you to call John Singer Sargent and you couldn't find him in the Rolodex?"

Pietro asks all the applicants these questions, and many more, but these three seem to really separate the wheat from the chaff.

One applicant in particular rises to the top. Her name is Marjorie. Her hair is short, styled in the career fashion some women do nowadays. She must have become accustomed to wearing it that way while serving as a first lieutenant in the Women's Army Corps during World War II. She has already been working as a secretary at MIT in another department for over a decade after the war, so she knows the ins and outs of the university's bureaucracy.

Marjorie lists that she has a good memory on her resume, and because people sometimes sneak things on there that they never expect anyone to double check, Pietro asks her all three of his perfunctory questions in rapid-fire succession without waiting for a response. It turns the interview into more of an interrogation, but Pietro wants to see how she handles the pressure, especially because he'd like to keep his own anxiety to a minimum.

Marjorie looks at Pietro curiously for a moment, then says with little affect, "I don't speak Italian, but I can quote opera lyrics as a party trick. Both of my hands are normal length, thank you. And I'd give you my condolences because John Singer Sargent has been dead for thirty-five years. Although I could get a medium on the line, if you'd like."

Pietro tilts his head to the side, considering whether she's actually serious.

"The second one is a joke," Marjorie explains. "My shorthand is quite good."

Pietro holds back a laugh. The interrogation isn't over. "And why do you want to work for me?"

"Your answer is in the question. Because then I'd be working for you, Pietro Belluschi, the world-renowned architect. Sounds a lot more exciting than what I'm doing right now."

"But I don't want it to be exciting."

"Then I'll make it dreadfully dreary for you and keep the excitement to myself."

Pietro bursts out laughing.

"I suppose that means I lost the job," Marjorie says with a straight face, which only causes Pietro to laugh even more.

There's something about this woman. She makes a strong first impression, but Pietro will be spending a lot of time around her.

"How do you feel about long hours?"

"As long as they're nice to me, I'll be nice to them."

Pietro smirks. "I . . . want to make sure we'll get along . . . socially. As my secretary, you'll be accountable for aspects of both my professional and personal lives. Keeping my calendar and so forth."

"That's the job description. So . . . what would you like to know? Have I read any good books lately? Do I like to watch movies?"

"Well, do you?"

"Watch movies? Yes. I find movies are much better when you watch them."

Pietro smiles. "Have you seen any good ones recently?"

Marjorie searches her memory. "No, but I would like to see this new one, *Messalina*. It's playing at the Brattle in Cambridge. Have you heard of it?"

"*Messalina* . . . That name sounds familiar."

"It might if you've read *I, Claudius*. It's that book about that Roman emperor."

Pietro shakes his head in disbelief, trying to remember. "She's the one who marries Claudius, isn't she?"

"That's right. I can't wait to see how they treat her in the story." Marjorie throws up her hands. "Even though they never get women right in the movies. They're always as two-dimensional as the screen."

"Maybe they should put someone like you up there instead."

"Me? No, I'm too good-looking to be a movie star."

Pietro knows she's trying to be self-deprecating, but the joke doesn't work. Marjorie is quite stunning. Or at least Pietro feels stunned, sensing that sort of possession beautiful women often inflict.

"Would you like to go?" Marjorie asks. "See if we could watch a movie together. Socially?"

Pietro presses his lips together. It's an unconventional idea, but perhaps a good one.

"You said it was at the Brattle?" Pietro asks.

"Yes. They have the best popcorn."

Helen likes the popcorn at the Brattle. She started coming here when the theatre opened. They still lived in Cambridge then. Those were simpler times. She'd eat a tub all on her own, only sharing it when the boys were in town. The Brattle is only a subway ride away, so she still makes the trek to the theatre sometimes, to the popcorn, to simpler times.

Sometimes she arrives a half hour early to make sure she doesn't miss any previews. And there's always something good to see. Last year there was *Ben-Hur* and *Some Like It Hot*, and now there's this new film, *Messsalina*. Helen remembers the name from that book Pietro used to talk about. When they used to talk about books. When they used to talk.

Perhaps if the film is good enough, Pietro would like to come see it with her.

Then again, it probably won't be a very entertaining show. And you never know what type of crowd these theatres are attracting nowadays.

When Helen arrives at the box office, she sees a couple buying their tickets. It looks like young love, even though she sees the man isn't very young.

Helen eyes them as they go inside and get a tub of popcorn. They're probably going to share it, aren't they? Because it seems like popcorn isn't the only thing they're sharing.

Should Helen get some popcorn? Drown it in butter? Drown her problems?

No, the more she thinks about it, the more she knows popcorn isn't the answer. She should just go home.

Because even if she did like the popcorn and the movie, she doesn't think she can stomach the preview.

Chapter Thirty

THE CONFESSIONAL

If you pray long enough, something will always come to you. Or at least that's what Pietro hopes will happen. He clasps his hands together. Squeezes them. Strangles the air.

Pietro only separates his hands to loosen his tie. His Windsor knot acts more like a noose. And he can't let it choke him. There has already been too much death. The Grim Reaper surrounds Pietro, hides around every corner with his black cloak and sickle, ready to pounce. Pietro prays for a reprieve.

A man in black sits next to Pietro. Just because he is wearing a suit doesn't mean he is not the Grim Reaper. You'd like to think you could recognize the Grim Reaper when he sits beside you, but Pietro can hardly recognize this man.

"What are you praying for?" the man asks.

Pietro glances over, then shuts his eyes. "I pray because that's what you do when someone dies."

"I meant," the man continues, "*who* are you praying for?"

"Then you should have chosen your words more carefully."

The man stands up and walks a short distance away, then

stops himself. Or at least something stops him. Perhaps it's the same thing Pietro is praying for: some sign, or a spirit.

Or perhaps it's the spires. There are seven in the chapel. The man takes in the vaulted, triangular ceilings. The spiky, spired ceiling looks like something out of a sci-fi novel. But it's not entirely otherworldly. It's an abstracted version of the mountains that surround the chapel. And there is something about it that's quite formidable, impenetrable. That's probably why the Air Force Academy chose this design for its Cadet Chapel. Pietro was a design consultant on the project, but his name isn't on the finished product.

Being the newest of the Armed Forces, the Air Force has its sights set on the horizon more than any other branch. Human flight was a pipe dream when this country was founded and now we can move through the air faster than sound. There is always something around the corner, over the horizon, and it is the Air Force's job to prepare its cadets for that future.

But there is always something you can't prepare someone for: What comes after war. What comes after loss. You can put a plane back together, or build a new one. But it's harder to do that with a soul.

Pietro had to put his pieces back together after the Great War. He remembers his room. He remembers Rimbaud. And he remembers praying. Hopefully, praying will help with the war currently raging inside him.

The man sits back down next to Pietro. "You're praying for her, aren't you?"

Pietro nods but doesn't open his eyes. Yes, he's here to pray for

Helen. She wasn't able to survive the war inside her. She started drinking, but she wasn't drinking to get drunk. Some medicine comes in a pill and some comes in a bottle. Some comes from a doctor and some comes from the corner store. Liquor can be both a sickness and a symptom. And even though it's never a cure, that won't stop people from trying it just to make sure.

Pietro opens his eyes, but not for long.

He wouldn't want Helen to see the man he's become. The Pan Am Building is nearing completion, but what was supposed to be his crowning achievement has made him into a pariah. Citizens and critics deride the design, calling it an eyesore, determined the building was a blatant cash grab, both for the developers and the architects.

Pietro's lips part and he whispers, "'It is easier for a camel to go through the eye of a needle than for someone who is rich to enter the kingdom of God.'"

The man leans in. "I'm sorry, I didn't hear what you said."

Pietro opens his eyes and scans the ceiling. "My name isn't on this building. And I wish my name wasn't on *that* one either."

The man dips his head. "You're still beating yourself up about that too?"

Pietro turns to him. "A few suggestions. Here and there. That's all they really wanted me for. That, and my name. And Gropius's. Made it an easy job, really, for both of us. But . . . I hope it's not my last one. It could be, you know. Probably shouldn't even attend the opening. Don't want my name associated with that building even more than it already is. They should have given the project to Pei. The building he designed was . . . Well, it was glorious. But . . . they would have found a way to ruin it. They would have said the curves were . . . too curvy. 'Why don't you make them straight?' And he didn't need the job anyway. No, his career is ahead of him—not behind, like mine. He's going to do great things. He *is* doing great things, really. I made sure of that. I was on the committee for the new JFK Library. And we gave it to him, on my recommendation. So, he's going to do well. Quite well, indeed." Pietro cups his head in his hands. "Unlike me. Unlike —" But he can't say Helen's name. Pietro throws up his hands. "Unlike Jackie Kennedy." Pietro's eyelids attempt to mimic a dam, but there's a breach. "She's such a lovely woman, you know. It's such a shame . . . such a shame what happened. It really is. No one should ever be put in a position like that. You spend your entire life . . . You have something so beautiful with someone . . . And then it's all taken away from you." Pietro wipes the tears from his eyes.

The man takes Pietro's hand. "So, this is where they put the confessional. Odd placement, really, right here in a pew instead of somewhere off to the side."

The air tumbles out of Pietro's lungs. For a moment it turns into a laugh, but he chokes it back. Pietro eyes the man in black, holding his hand tightly.

It's such an odd sort of torture. Having children, that is—especially for an architect. Architecture is all about control, and having children is all about letting go. Except with children, letting go happens slowly. You give them bit after bit of independence until they're someone you could never imagine. Until they're . . . sitting beside you, holding your hand, a magnificent man you can hardly recognize even if he's your son, Tony.

"A wise man once told me," Tony says, "that a wise man once told him . . . that what a man needs is a good book."

"Good book? I guess there's no better location, or time, to give me a Bible."

But Tony doesn't hand him a Bible. Instead, he hands Pietro a copy of *The Agony and the Ecstasy*, a novel about Michelangelo painting the ceiling of the Sistine Chapel.

"Ah," Pietro says. "I think I might have said something more along the lines of finding your own muses . . . but I think you got the gist."

Tony's eyes twinkle. "And I know you said it would be more meaningful if the muses come from you and your experiences, but because I'm . . . well, I thought maybe we could share this experience together."

Pietro sets the book to his side. "I think that's a fine idea." He clasps his hands together. "But for now, I think there's something else we need to do."

Tony takes his cue. Father and son pray.

Then it comes.

Chapter Thirty-One

THE AGONY AND THE ECSTASY

"To try to understand another human being, to grapple for his ultimate depths, that is the most dangerous of human endeavors."

—Irving Stone, *The Agony and the Ecstasy*

Irving Stone is right to lump agony and ecstasy together, describing not only the act of creation, but humanity itself. We can go from the depths of agony to the depths of ecstasy, the full range of human emotion, in a matter of seconds. The mind can be a race car, zooming from one to another with reckless abandon. Sometimes, though, agony and ecstasy aren't separate emotions, but a singular one smashed together like metal in a car crash.

Pietro doesn't like to drive. He prefers the train, at least when he has an engrossing novel to read. There's something calming, soothing, about reading a book on a train. Something about the world zooming past while you explore it through someone else's point of view. It makes reading all the more intoxicating.

Pietro doesn't like to imbibe liquor while he's reading. A cup of tea is all he needs to drink with a book. Not too much, mind you, but enough to keep his mind concentrated on the pages in front of him instead of the world around him. That's not too hard to understand.

The danger in the exercise of understanding another human being is less easy, harder to pinpoint. Perhaps the statement itself says more about Irving than anything else. Perhaps that's the point.

The Agony and the Ecstasy begins with Michelangelo examining his faults in a mirror. We rarely like to see our worst qualities reflected back at us, but the faults Michelangelo lists are only the ones on the surface, only the ones others can easily see. Beneath the surface, beneath the skin, beneath the tissue, resides the real issue: there are emotions inside us we don't want to see reflected back. So, we find other things to attack.

If we truly come to an understanding about the faults in others, then we might have to wrangle the faults in ourselves to understand the person behind the reflection and the emotion that stirs up.

Pietro has had his share of agony, not only in his personal life but in his professional one too. He doesn't know if he can deal with the emotion dredging all that up might incur, but he can't help but try to understand Michelangelo. Pietro can see himself in Michelangelo's shoes, struggling for respect, struggling for his legacy. But why does Michelangelo's legacy matter to him so much? Is it something another project, even something as grand as the Sistine Chapel, could satisfy?

If only Pietro could have something like that. One more

project . . . that's all he needs to set the course of his career straight.

While traveling by train might be great for reading books, it's not the best for staying in contact with your office. Upon his arrival back in Boston, Marjorie has a surprise for Pietro.

"Actually, it's more like three surprises," she says. Not one, but three big commissions have come in for Pietro. The first is for the Rohm and Haas headquarters in Philadelphia, the next is for the Bank of America Tower in San Francisco, and the last is for the Cathedral of St. Mary of the Assumption, also in San Francisco.

All three are major commissions. Each in its own way has the capacity to put Pietro back on the map, but therein lies part of the problem. There are three projects stretched across America, one on the East Coast and two on the West. How will he ever manage them all, even with other architectural offices taking up the slack?

Pietro still has to find the inspiration for each project, that special something beyond what the client can provide. He needs to listen to the clients' needs, but he can't let them dictate the designs. He's learned that lesson. So, where will he find that extra bit of inspiration?

Wherever he can.

Rohm and Haas's principal product is plexiglass, a shatter-resistant alternative to glass. So, Pietro uses the company's marvel of science to create sun shades to reduce the building's air conditioning load. It not only serves as a practical advance, but it imbues the building with the whole soul of the enterprise, not merely giving the company a showpiece for its product, but a way to display its corporate identity and the possibilities plexiglass can provide.

For the Bank of America Tower, Pietro goes back to his favorite source of inspiration: nature. He camps out in the Cascade Mountains amongst the great basaltic formations. A human is like an ant next to these towering stones. If Pietro were an ant, the formations might look like sticks clumped together in a bundle. Pietro burns a bundle of wood to keep him cozy as he camps near a lake, trying to cook up his dinner along with an idea or two.

Nature sculpts all its surfaces, but there is something about these basaltic formations that stretches into the human realm. The sharp edges resemble buildings, skyscrapers stacked against each other, an abstracted version of a skyline in the same way the Air Force Academy Cadet Chapel is an abstracted version of mountains.

So, what if instead of trying to design one building in a skyline, one column in a formation, Pietro uses the entire skyline to make one building? The entire formation to make one column? Put another way, he could use their natural style, the design God has given us in these basaltic formations, for the Bank of America Tower. He could make the building out of a dark stone to complete the resemblance, but the windows would stand out like dark holes . . . unless he tints the glass so the reflection matches the masonry.

One after another, the ideas keep coming. The ecstasy of creation surges through him, flushing out the agony.

Pietro hires a young sculptor named Michio Ihara to make a

model of his design for the Bank of America Tower using sticks so that Pietro can play with the positioning to get the formation just right before it is set in Swedish granite. Pietro designs not only the building, though, but the plaza nearby, tapping another sculptor, Masayuki Nagare, to create an original art piece for it.

Swedish granite. A Japanese sculptor. The Bank of America. How very American.

Some mistake Nagare's sculpture as scornful. *The Banker's Heart*, they call it: a black heart sitting in front of a bank. But that's not the sculpture's name.

Pietro doesn't walk toward it; the sculpture pulls him forward. Two hundred tons of black granite creates its own gravity, drawing Pietro into its orbit. The closer Pietro gets to the sculpture, the more he can see himself in its highly polished surface, the more it becomes a mirror.

It's becoming easier to look at himself in the mirror these days. Two sculptors, one to help design the building and another to adorn it, both of Japanese descent. As Pietro looks at himself in the sculpture, he senses the agony and ecstasy crashing together inside him.

This heart is not black. It merely reflects the image of yourself that you give it. The closer you get to it, the closer you come to truly understanding yourself.

As Pietro pauses in front of the sculpture, he knows. This is no banker's heart.

It's his own.

Chapter Thirty-Two

TRANSCENDENCE

Transcendence is the true name of Nagare's sculpture. But the name could apply to any artwork, because the true purpose of art is to allow you to perceive something beyond what can be seen. The meaning of the work transcends its physical form. In that way, art is like God. Or scripture. Its meaning lies beyond what you can touch or read, requiring an act of faith.

Michelangelo recognized the pressure of creating art that transcends its physical form, transcends its representation of reality. He had to paint the ceiling of the Sistine Chapel, the ceiling God reaches through to ordain new popes. But Michelangelo didn't build the Sistine Chapel—he only decorated the ceiling, whereas Pietro must design the entire church.

How can you create a sense of transcendence in architecture, especially when the purpose of that architecture is to bring people closer to God? The stakes are as high as heaven. Success leads to salvation; failure leads to damnation. At least that's the way it seems to Pietro's ulcers.

The site for the Cathedral of St. Mary of the Assumption

is only a thirty-minute walk from the Bank of America Tower, but it seems worlds apart. Pietro has designed churches before, but something about this one escapes his grasp, eludes his comprehension.

"Artists are the antennas of any given age," Pietro tells Marjorie. "My antenna must be broken."

"Maybe you need to tune into a different station?"

"Seems like that's what *they're* about to do," Pietro responds. "The church has already burned through three different architects." Pietro paces. "I should reject the commission. They're just going to burn me next."

"Come on, now," Marjorie says. "No architect in his right mind would refuse a job like this."

Pietro stops pacing. "Does it look like I'm in my right mind?"

"I'm sorry. Is your mind your antenna in this scenario?" Marjorie asks dryly.

Pietro sighs. "My antenna should be melted down. Then it could be put to some good use."

Marjorie crosses her arms. "Seems like you're already melting down."

Pietro purses his lips, narrows his eyes. "When I take a job, I listen. That's what gets me the job, and that's what allows me to keep it. But they want seating for two and a half thousand people in the nave. And they can't be too far from the altar, mind you, if you want people to hear. That means there can only be, I don't know, give or take somewhere around seventeen rows of pews distributed in an array around the altar."

"An array? Like a radio array?"

Pietro narrows his eyes. "What do you mean, a radio array?"

"Not to belabor your antenna metaphor too much," Marjorie starts, "but a radio array is a collection of smaller antennas that work together to create a much bigger antenna."

"Perhaps, but . . . what does any of that have to do with this?"

"Perhaps your antenna isn't the problem," Marjorie says. "It's the fact that you're not strengthening your signal with other people's antennas. I read that book you mentioned, by the way. *The Agony and the Ecstasy*. The story of Michelangelo, the lone wolf, the solitary artist. It's quite amorous, actually, in how it romanticizes this masculine notion of the artist who doesn't need anyone's help. He only needs to be left alone to commune with his genius." Marjorie rolls her eyes. "It's a bunch of rubbish, if you ask me. You don't work alone; you partner with others. So why aren't you right now? Eduardo Catalano sent his new book over. You worked with him on Juilliard, didn't you? Why don't you see if something in his book strikes your fancy? Because if you're just going to blab on and on like this, then I . . . will tune out."

Marjorie punctuates the end of her speech by handing over a copy of Catalano's *Structures of Warped Surfaces*.

Pietro holds it in his hands, inspecting the back cover before raising his eyes to meet Marjorie's. "Don't take my acceptance of this book as acceptance of the way you just spoke to me," Pietro says. "But . . . thank you."

Pietro enjoys working with Marjorie too much to get rid of

her. And she's right, he enjoys working with other people too much to be so blind to this creative block.

Pietro reads Catalano's book, looking for inspiration. But a book is no substitute for a man, so he calls Catalano on the phone.

"Have you seen pictures of Kenzō Tange's St. Mary's Cathedral in Tokyo?" Pietro asks.

"And here I thought you were calling to congratulate me on my work," Catalano says.

"Actually, I was calling to see if you wanted some more work. Maybe design a ceiling with me using hyperbolic paraboloids. Maybe show Tange how it's done?"

If you ever need to make an appeal to an architect, it's best to appeal directly to their competitiveness.

Pietro and Catalano work together on the design. It's a similar octagonal shape to the Portsmouth Abbey, but instead of a straightforward, eight-sided structure that anyone could build, they envision a monumental cathedral with eight warped walls, all hyperbolic paraboloids folding in on each other, soaring up into the air to a vaulted ceiling, culminating in a cross. And unlike Tange's cathedral, the congregation will see out into the city, because the vaulted ceiling is suspended on four concrete pylons, allowing Pietro and Catalano to install floor-to-ceiling windows on all sides. It's a brilliant, bold design. Or at least it will be, if they can make it work structurally.

"I think we need to extend our array," Pietro tells Catalano. He says they need to bring in a structural engineer, and there's no one better than Pier Luigi Nervi, especially when working with reinforced concrete.

"I think you need to come to Italy," Nervi tells them.

"You want us to study the Pantheon?" Pietro responds. "Study its concrete dome, like I did in school?"

"You can, if you like," Nervi says. "But there's a lab in Bergamo that would probably be better."

Pietro and Catalano hop on the next flight to Italy. They take up residence at the Bergamo Testing Laboratory, a lab that specializes in testing concrete. Together with Nervi, they build a model of their design, but it's not some tabletop prop. It's a two-hundred-square-foot architectural model built to see if their design can withstand the elements, including any earthquakes San Francisco could throw at it.

But the model develops cracks, shows its own fault lines. So, they build a new model. Then another one. Then another one. Then another one. The months and monoliths go by. They're about to lose their nerve, but then Nervi cracks the construction, coming up with a solution so they can keep their curves.

"The dome sits on four legs," Nervi says. "So, what if we extend those legs into the ground with cables? All the way down below the surface of the ground."

It's always convenient when you can bury your problems in the ground. But this solution is sound. All they have to do now is assure the wary city engineers of San Francisco, and whatever redevelopment review boards they'll convene—besides convincing a conservative archbishop to embrace their radical design.

Luckily for the archbishop, Pietro only has to put his array on display and show him that what he's proposing isn't that radical at all, especially compared to the hippies at the corner of Ashbury and Haight, or wherever those radicals hang out.

Pietro introduces the archbishop to Enrico Manfrini, an Italian sculptor who will make the church's doors look like the ones Lorenzo Ghiberti designed for the Baptistry in Florence. The archbishop knows which ones he's talking about. Then Pietro shows him pictures of what he and Richard Lippold did at the Portsmouth Abbey Church. But not to worry, Richard won't do some completely abstract design. He'll make a contemporary version of the baldachin, the canopy over the altar, that Gian Lorenzo Bernini designed for St. Peter's in Rome. It's all very traditional, if you think about it . . .

They say it takes more muscles to smile than to frown. So how many does it take to keep a straight face?

When completed, Lippold's aluminum centerpiece captures light from the multicolored stained-glass windows above and shoots it out across the nave. There's nothing traditional about it, except that it is beautiful. And beauty is timeless. Transcendent, you could say. But then again, as with all art, some things are better left unsaid.

Chapter Thirty-Three

IF I WERE A WOMAN . . .

"If I were a woman, I'd always be pregnant," Pietro tells Marjorie, simultaneously complaining and bragging about how busy he is.

"Let's say, for both our sakes . . . we're lucky that's not the case."

A corporate office, then a skyscraper, and finally, a shrine to the Lord. Pietro has repeatedly shown he can design anything. And not only has he wiped his slate clean from the Pan Am Building, but he's shown he is an architect to be reckoned with.

With the success of these three projects—especially the Rohm and Haas building, which was rapidly constructed—Pietro knows it's his opportunity to branch out. He no longer needs the nest of MIT to bolster his bona fides.

"I think there's some saying about a fish and a pond that applies to this scenario," Marjorie remarks.

"I thought it was more like the story of Christ feeding the multitude," Pietro says, "with the never-ending tide of projects I sign on to."

"I don't think that's an apt comparison at all," Marjorie says. "Jesus doesn't have anywhere near the same level of ego as you do."

Pietro laughs, but he has a hard time looking at Marjorie. She's come to mean so much more to him than she could ever be as his secretary. She's family. Or at least he wants her to be.

"You know, I have been thinking about making a few changes," Pietro says.

"I'm no good at picking out wallpaper, if you're thinking of redecorating the office."

Pietro bites his lip. "No, it's not—well . . . I guess it sort of is an office redecoration, of sorts."

"A new desk, then?"

"No, I . . . I'm thinking about stepping down as dean."

"That's an odd way of telling me I'm fired."

Pietro exhales. "No, you're not fired."

"I'll make sure I clear that up at the unemployment office."

Pietro scratches his neck. "Actually, I don't want you to stop working for me."

"I'm fired and then I get a job offer on the same day. I guess it's my turn to get in on some of that 'feeding the multitude' action. What do you want me to do? I do have my driver's license, so I could be your chauffeur, but I do have to warn you . . . I bribed the proctor who gave me my driving test."

"Well, it's not quite a job."

Marjorie lifts her chin. "I'm a little old for an internship, if that's what you're trying to pull."

"I'm not trying to pull anything," Pietro reassures her. "I'm trying to bend something, though."

"Bend me to your will?"

"Actually," Pietro says as he bends down on one knee, "I was wondering if you'd like to be my wife."

Marjorie narrows her eyes. "I'm sorry. Are you firing me or are you asking me to marry you?"

"I guess . . . both, actually." Pietro furrows his brow. "Now that I think about it."

"So, let me get this straight. You don't want me to work for you anymore."

"Yes, that's right."

"But you do want me to work for you. Only, it won't be a job."

"Uh . . . yes."

"So I'll be doing the same work."

"I think so."

"You just won't be paying me."

"I guess not."

Marjorie tilts her head to the side. "But . . . instead of receiving my own paycheck, I'll get to spend all *your* money."

Pietro's voice is shaky. "I'm not quite sure that's a part of—"

"Were you planning on having a prenuptial agreement?"

"Well, I hadn't thought about—"

"They're not very romantic."

Pietro twists the watch on his wrist. "No, I don't suppose we will, then."

"That's good," Marjorie says coyly. She looks off into the distance, lost in thought.

Pietro looks around. "Should I stay on one knee, or . . ."

"Oh!" Marjorie says, popping back to the room. "Remind me, why are you on one knee?"

Pietro rocks in place. "Because I'm asking you to marry me."

"That's a good question," Marjorie says. "But perhaps a better one would be, do you want me to be your wife?"

"Yes, I thought that was obvious."

Marjorie clutches her hands together, bounces on her feet. "Even after everything . . . All this . . . that I put you through?"

Pietro nods. "I do."

"Well . . . then I do too. I guess."

Pietro gets off his knee. "God bless." He embraces Marjorie, then kisses her.

Marjorie's mouth is slack when she steps back. She sucks in a quick breath of air before going back in. Now it's her turn to kiss him. She caresses his face, running her thumb across his moustache when their lips part. "I guess I'll have to get used to that, won't I?"

"I hope so."

"How long do I have to plan the wedding? I need much longer than two weeks' notice, if that's what you were thinking."

Pietro smiles. "When would you like to get married?"

"So, now I have to make all the decisions?"

Pietro's eyes go wide. "What? I—"

But she shuts him up with a kiss. "It never ceases to amaze me how gullible you are sometimes."

Pietro looks down, then back at Marjorie. "I think—" he starts, but he can't keep her eyeline. "I think it's because I trust you."

Marjorie runs her thumb across his moustache again. "Sucker," she says, punctuating the sentiment with a smooch.

Happy wife. Happy life.

Happy wife. No strife.

Happy wife. Love is rife.

These sentiments are true, regardless of how insipid they might be. Pietro can't help but write them all down, one after another, day after day, as if he's internalizing them.

His marriage to Marjorie is fast approaching. Pietro wants her to be happy. And he knows his last wife wasn't.

As Pietro prepares his vows, he thinks about what vows mean. They're a solemn promise, not only to your betrothed, but to God. Ephesians 5:25 says, "For husbands, marriage means love your wives, just as Christ loved the church. He gave up his life for her." You must sacrifice everything for your wife, give yourself to her fully.

Pietro reads that Bible verse to her during his vows. And Marjorie responds with her own, quoting 1 Peter 4:8, "Above all, love each other deeply, because love covers over a . . . multitude . . . of sins." Marjorie winks at him.

She keeps her end of the bargain. She loves Pietro deeply. And if it's true that it's easier for a camel to go through the eye of a needle than for a rich man to enter the kingdom of God, then Marjorie does everything in her power to make Pietro a pauper.

~

Eight years go by in the blink of an eye. Pietro keeps his promise. Marjorie keeps hers too, along with a few things she picks up at the department store.

But life doesn't always turn out the way you expect it to. Or at least it doesn't for Dr. Burkes. Dr. Burkes dies of cancer, the same cancer that took his daughter. Genevieve now lives all alone in the house she helped design for her family.

It's a beautiful, sunny day in May when Pietro catches up with Genevieve in her darkest hour. She runs her hands along the rhododendrons she once planted with her husband as she leads Pietro on a little reunion tour of the place.

"I don't think I can stay here any longer," she says. "And I don't think I can sell the house to anyone but you."

Pietro's shoulders curl over his chest, his heart breaking for hers.

"I know that's not much of a sales pitch," Genevieve says.

Pietro sweats. Marjorie's spending is a drop in the bucket compared to the downpour this house will cost, but Pietro knows how much love went into its construction.

Pietro bends his neck. "I don't know what I'd do if I ever lost Marjorie."

Genevieve touches his shoulder.

"I'll take it . . . on one condition," Pietro says. "You come up every now and again to help us trim these rhododendrons. There are some things no one should have to do on their own."

Chapter Thirty-Four

ANONYMOUS ENTRY 1026

"I'm sorry, ma'am. Can I see your ID?"

But Maya Lin doesn't need to fish out her driver's license; she has it ready. She hands it to the bartender.

"Twenty-one," the bartender says, then taps it in his hand. "This isn't a fake, is it?"

"No . . . it's real," she's says, exhaling. By now, Maya is used to men hemming and hawing over her qualifications. And that's why she needs a drink. Especially right now. Why on earth would Pietro Belluschi want to get a drink with her?

"Ms. Lin," Pietro says as he sidles up next to the bar.

"Mr. Belluschi," Maya says as she shakes his hand. "Please call me Maya."

"And please call me anytime you like," Pietro says. "But when you do, please call me Pietro."

Maya smiles.

"I'm sorry," Pietro says. "Sometimes I get my wife's voice in my head. What she says off the cuff is often more interesting than anything I have to say." Pietro turns to the bartender. "Whiskey, neat."

The bartender pours. There's no need for a man Pietro's age to show his ID. It's written on his face.

"Thank you for meeting me," Pietro says to Maya.

"Thank you for . . . asking me. It's the least I can do after you selected me for the memorial."

It's 1981, and Pietro was on the jury committee that selected Maya's design for the Vietnam Veterans Memorial. All submissions were anonymous, numbered. Maya's was entry number 1,026.

"Yes, I suppose I should apologize about that," Pietro says, then clears his throat.

The bartender hands over their drinks. Two whiskeys, neat.

"I see we have the same drink," Pietro says.

"I guess it's not surprising we have a similar palate, considering," Maya says as she holds up her glass. "Cheers."

They clink glasses. Pietro takes a sip. Maya downs hers in one go, then nods to the bartender.

Pietro grins. "You do have wonderful taste."

"Do I, though? Or am I just lucky?"

Pietro takes another sip. "Luck doesn't explain your eloquence. How you bridged the earth with the sky, reminding us to remember the dead buried in the ground. Each name is a message, a meditation."

"Seems like you're the one who's eloquent, not me." The bartender hands over Maya's drink. She takes a swig. "All I did was draw attention to the ground."

"Perhaps we should sit down," Pietro says.

Maya joins Pietro at a table nearby. She takes another swig.

Pietro clasps his hands together. "There's no need to denigrate your design."

"Why not? Everyone else is."

"Yes, well, I know a thing or two about weathering a storm of criticism."

"You mean the Pan Am Building?"

Now it's Pietro's turn to drink. "I see my reputation precedes me."

Maya shifts in her seat. "Well, you still received an AIA Gold Medal. Congratulations, by the way."

"That was a long time ago. And it was controversial," Pietro says, tapping his glass with his finger, "because of my reputation."

Maya wrinkles her nose. "As controversial as when you gave it to Wright?"

Pietro smiles. "I almost forgot about that." He savors the memory with his next sip. "It's becoming harder and harder to remember things like that, you know—the good things. That's why I try not to recall the politics of it all." He nods toward Maya. "Unless there's a good reason."

Maya crosses her arms. "So, are you here to get me to change the design, like everyone else?"

Pietro chuckles. "I can't tell you what to do. You won. We chose you. Hell, I never won a design competition in my life. Only ever entered one: 1935, the Oregon State Capitol competition. And I lost—badly." Pietro clenches his jaw. "No, you need to do whatever you think is right."

Pietro slowly sips his whiskey. So does Maya. She opens her mouth a bit before confiding, "You know, my entry, it was a project for a class. And I got a B on it."

Pietro grins. "I thought I heard something like that."

"But you know what?" Maya starts. "The professor who gave me that B? He entered the competition too. And I beat him."

"Cheers to that," Pietro says. They clink glasses. "Sometimes people don't recognize your brilliance." Pietro takes another swallow.

Maya swallows as well, but it's not whiskey. She's trying to build up the type of courage whiskey can't provide. She leans forward. "Would you have selected me if you . . . knew who I was?"

"You mean, because you're a woman? An Asian woman? A young Asian woman who hasn't even graduated college yet?"

"That seems to be the list of qualities that comes up the most often," Maya responds.

Pietro presses his lips together. "I won't lie and say it never crossed my mind," he says. "But you have more formal architectural training than Brunelleschi did when he designed Il Duomo, so who am I to say? When I was younger, I would have said you need to choose the best architect for a project, not merely the best design. Because architecture isn't about drawing. Well, it is about that, but it's also about what you're willing to sacrifice to achieve your vision. It's about the politics of it all . . . as you've recently become aware. But it's too much turbulence, if you ask me. That's why I don't fly anymore either. Too much turbulence. Too much jostling." Pietro shakes his hands in the air for effect.

"I used to be a firehorse," he continues. "Do you know what that is? It's a horse that used to pull the cart to fight a fire before, you know, fire engines came around. And I'm like that firehorse: used to the action, can't settle down in the barn. But I've learned a thing or two in the barn. There's always something, someone better who comes along. The firehorse can't imagine the fire engine. And I think some architects have a lack of imagination . . . about who should be an architect."

Maya smiles quickly, then stares down at her hands.

Pietro swallows. "I'm sorry that businessman Ross Perot called you an 'egg roll' or whatever nonsense came out of his mouth."

Maya nods. "Thank you."

"I don't know whatever personal demons he's dealing with, but he's not even an architect, so you shouldn't listen to anything he says. Old horses like him and me are going to die one of these days and all that'll be left will be you fire engines. That's what makes your memorial so . . . I'm sorry, Marjorie says I ramble too much."

"No, please," Maya says graciously. "Sometimes it's good to listen to someone else's thoughts. Allows me to escape my own."

"Well, that's why I love your memorial so much." Pietro sets down his drink. "A memorial isn't about the past. I mean, it *is* about the past, but it's about how we *live* with the past."

Maya perks up. "And how we live with the things we've done and the people we lost," she says.

Pietro nods, then lowers his head. "Sometimes, when I look back on my work, the things I've done . . . I didn't have the imagination I should have. I concentrated too much on what I thought was reason and didn't allow enough room for sheer imagination, for fantasy, if that makes sense."

Maya's eyes are soft. "My favorite work of yours is St. Mary's. You can't tell me you weren't filled with . . ." she says, searching for the right words, "the spirit of fantasy and imagination when you did that."

Pietro reaches for his glass, but stops short and wipes his eye. "You're too kind to an old man."

"It's the least I can do. You've been so kind to me."

"To be honest," Pietro says, "I feared you might judge me too harshly, like a book you might discard if it has an odd turn of phrase, instead of looking deeper into its spine, into the content, the depth of ideas expressed." Pietro downs the rest of his drink. "Which brings me to our next point of order, really."

Maya blinks, raises her eyebrows. "And what's that?"

"You're a bright young woman. You must know all the bright young things."

"I suppose you could say that."

"Do you know anyone who might want to write my memoirs?"

Chapter Thirty-Five

THE REQUIEM

There is something funereal about organ music—regardless of the melody—but it's even more maudlin when it's Mozart's Requiem. Mozart didn't orchestrate his Requiem for the organ, but that's not stopping the man in the white suit from playing it.

Whoever's idea it was for him to perform it before the screening of the film *Amadeus* at the Paramount Theatre in Portland . . . should be commended. You've never heard the section "Dies Irae," otherwise known as "The Day of Wrath," unless you've heard someone furiously pound it into a pipe organ.

Whoever's idea it was for the performance, though, Marjorie gets credit for bringing Pietro there, surprising him by taking him to a screening of this film adaptation of the *Mozart and Salieri* opera Pietro fell in love with all those years ago. More precisely, it's an adaptation of Peter Shaffer's stage play, but you can track all these tales back to Mozart's widow Constanze. She was the first person charged with floating the idea that Mozart got the commission for the Requiem composition from a mysterious stranger, all the while becoming increasingly paranoid that he might be writing his own requiem.

Does anyone really care that it was Count Franz von Walsegg who commissioned the piece to commemorate his wife's death? There's no story there. And it's the story Pietro loves about the film. There's the grumpy, begrudging Salieri, nervous about his legacy and how he'll be perceived now that God's favor is shining on someone else. Instead of basking in Mozart's brilliance, Salieri schemes to demolish him. He's such an unreliable, nasty sod. Absolutely riveting to watch, though, especially with F. Murray Abraham's performance. Salieri gazes at Mozart with admiration and devastation. All through the same set of eyes. Salieri is a thrilling person to watch, but a chilling person to be. Does it really matter that the real Salieri was a fan of Mozart's? And not only a fan, but a collaborator?

Pietro still hasn't found someone to write his memoirs. He wonders if, when the time comes, posterity will see him as a Mozart . . . or a Salieri.

"You have to get your ego under a bushel," Pietro would always say to a young architect if they were imitating Roark too much. Sometimes, though, the architect he needed to dress down was himself. Not everyone can be a Mozart, but the absolute worst thing to be is a jealous Salieri, tearing down others instead of building them up. Pietro is an architect, not a demolition expert, and he has tried to build up those around him.

But what will Pietro's legacy be? When Mozart died, they buried him in an anonymous grave, not knowing the extent to which he would be immortalized. When the time comes, Pietro knows Marjorie, his Constanze, will remember him. First *Messalina*, and now this film . . . Pietro knows there was a reason he fell in love with her.

Then there are his sons, their grandchildren, all the people who use his buildings, in their own way, and all the architects he has helped along the way—including two more recently in Los Angeles, Robert Kennard and Harold Williams.

Now, these men didn't really need any help from Pietro other than his name, but he was elated to lend it. These two highly qualified architects had already completed the design for the State Office Building in Van Nuys, California, but they couldn't win the commission unless they had another architect involved. It couldn't be any architect, though. While it would be wonderful if the architect they brought on was well known, someone like Pietro, it was more important that this person shared Pietro's skin tone. Robert Kennard and Harold Williams are Black and apparently the only black the commissioners cared about was Pietro's name, in ink, on the contract.

Pietro was glad to help them out, but sad he had to. America has made so much progress in Pietro's lifetime, and it's too bad that progress hasn't benefitted everyone equally, equitably. So many people still have prejudice in their hearts, deep-lingering hatred not unlike the kind Salieri has for anyone who gets any ounce of the recognition he thinks he deserves.

Perhaps what's worse, though, are the people who sit idly by when prejudice occurs. You can't always change the past, but you can do your part to turn the world into the place it should have been all along. It's up to us to build the future we want to live in. Pietro knows firsthand that confronting the sins of your past doesn't make you weak; it makes you stronger. True weakness is being blind to those sins, being complicit in them, passing the buck instead of building a world that doesn't depend on luck.

Years from now, even if Pietro is seen as a Salieri, maybe someday . . . someone will come along to write his memoirs, the literary version of his requiem. Or adapt his life story into something else. Maybe they'll do it in the same way Nikolai Rimsky-Korsakov and Peter Shaffer did with Salieri, turning him in a character, or a caricature, bringing him wider recognition, however infamous that recognition may be. Or maybe they'll try to capture Pietro's true essence. But even if they could, who knows if that would be engaging.

Only time will tell.

One man's ruse can be another man's muse.

Epilogue

"Let me end these brief confessions by saying that as there have been infinite visions of divine power, so there have been infinite ways of defining art or of creating meaningful architecture, which is the reason for their eternal appeal and continued renewal. The important thing is to recognize the problem as well as to recognize our own limitations. It is of some consolation to reflect that it is man's nature forever to search for new expressions in order to witness, though in imperfect ways, his own unique revelation of God and the mystery of his existence on earth."

—Pietro Belluschi

Pietro wrote these words on a slip of paper in a dog-eared copy of *David Copperfield* by Charles Dickens.

"Your father wanted me to give you this book," Marjorie says to Tony as they sit on a bench dedicated to Pietro in a park overlooking the city of Portland. Tony is fond of sitting on this hill with her. He looks forward to most of his trips to Portland, but his life is in Chicago. He's an architect, like his father, building his career on his own, away from the influence of his father's name. Pietro's passing left Marjorie all alone in the Burkes, now Belluschi, house.

"He kept reading it over and over again. Said he liked how it wasn't one big story. A little here, a little there. A series of vignettes. He said life's like that. Maybe not when you live it, but when you remember it. You can try to tell a complete story, but it doesn't always make sense." Marjorie hands over the book. "I don't know if this will help find someone for the memoirs, but it might."

Tony scans the slip of paper tucked into the margins, his eyes darting between the book and the horizon. "Whatever happened with Elisabeth?"

Marjorie tenses up. "She broke your father's heart, that's what she did."

"But . . . why did she stop working on it?"

Marjorie raises her eyebrows, gives Tony a glassy stare. "I don't think I ever got an answer."

Tony taps *David Copperfield* on his knee. "Maybe it's because he wanted his memoirs to have a . . . What would you call it? A literary flair?"

"When did he tell you that?"

"He didn't have to *tell* me. I read it, in his journal. There's some . . . entertaining stuff, but no one wants to tell someone else's story if you can't trust them."

Marjorie scoots toward Tony, throwing her arm around him. "Probably got that from your grandfather. Said he learned more about his father reading his memoirs than he did growing up with him."

"Well . . . here's hoping the same is true for me."

About the Author

W.A.W. Parker is an award-winning novelist, TV, and screenwriter in Los Angeles. His last novel *The Wasteland* won the American Fiction Award and the Foreword INDIES Book of the Year Award in LGBTQ+ Fiction. He grew up in northeastern Montana, an area the *Washington Post* has dubbed "the middle of nowhere," and then attended Harvard. He felt like Pietro Belluschi on his odd path to the Ivy League.

The Mentoris Project holds a special place in his heart, not only because they published his debut novel *The Divine Proportions of Luca Pacioli*, but because they allowed him to write this one—a novel about talent, ambition, and the American Dream . . . and how all of that, as you'll see, relates to his favorite film *Amadeus*.

ALSO FROM THE MENTORIS PROJECT

America's Forgotten Founding Father
A Novel Based on the Life of Filippo Mazzei
by Rosanne Welch, PhD

A. P. Giannini—Il Banchiere di Tutti
di Francesca Valente

A. P. Giannini—The People's Banker
by Francesca Valente

The Architect Who Changed Our World
A Novel Based on the Life of Andrea Palladio
by Pamela Winfrey

At Last
A Novel Based on the Life of Harry Warren
by Stacia Raymond

A Boxing Trainer's Journey
A Novel Based on the Life of Angelo Dundee
by Jonathan Brown

Breaking Barriers
A Novel Based on the Life of Laura Bassi
by Jule Selbo

Building Heaven's Ceiling
A Novel Based on the Life of Filippo Brunelleschi
by Joe Cline

Building Wealth
From Shoeshine Boy to Real Estate Magnate
by Robert Barbera

Building Wealth 101
How to Make Your Money Work for You
by Robert Barbera

Character is What Counts
A Novel Based on the Life of Vince Lombardi
by Jonathan Brown

Christopher Columbus: His Life and Discoveries
by Mario Di Giovanni

Dark Labyrinth
A Novel Based on the Life of Galileo Galilei
by Peter David Myers

Defying Danger
A Novel Based on the Life of Father Matteo Ricci
by Nicole Gregory

Desert Missionary
A Novel Based on the Life of Father Eusebio Kino
by Nicole Gregory

The Divine Proportions of Luca Pacioli
A Novel Based on the Life of Luca Pacioli
by W.A.W. Parker

The Dream of Life
A Novel Based on the Life of Federico Fellini
by Kate Fuglei

Dreams of Discovery
A Novel Based on the Life of the Explorer John Cabot
by Jule Selbo

The Embrace of Hope
A Novel Based on the Life of Frank Capra
by Kate Fuglei

The Faithful
A Novel Based on the Life of Giuseppe Verdi
by Collin Mitchell

Fermi's Gifts
A Novel Based on the Life of Enrico Fermi
by Kate Fuglei

First Among Equals
A Novel Based on the Life of Cosimo de' Medici
by Francesco Massaccesi

The Flesh and the Spirit
A Novel Based on the Life of St. Augustine of Hippo
by Sharon Reiser and Ali A. Smith

God's Messenger
A Novel Based on the Life of Mother Frances X. Cabrini
by Nicole Gregory

Grace Notes
A Novel Based on the Life of Henry Mancini
by Stacia Raymond

Guido's Guiding Hand
A Novel Inspired by the Life of Guido d'Arezzo
by Kinglsey Day

Harvesting the American Dream
A Novel Based on the Life of Ernest Gallo
by Karen Richardson

Humble Servant of Truth
A Novel Based on the Life of Thomas Aquinas
by Margaret O'Reilly

Leonardo's Secret
A Novel Based on the Life of Leonardo da Vinci
by Peter David Myers

Little by Little We Won
A Novel Based on the Life of Angela Bambace
by Peg A. Lamphier, PhD

The Making of a Prince
A Novel Based on the Life of Niccolò Machiavelli
by Maurizio Marmorstein

A Man of Action Saving Liberty
A Novel Based on the Life of Giuseppe Garibaldi
by Rosanne Welch, PhD

Marconi and His Muses
A Novel Based on the Life of Guglielmo Marconi
by Pamela Winfrey

No Person Above the Law
A Novel Based on the Life of Judge John J. Sirica
by Cynthia Cooper

The Pirate Prince of Genoa
A Novel Based on the Life of Admiral Andrea Doria
by Maurizio Marmorstein

Relentless Visionary: Alessandro Volta
by Michael Berick

Retire and Refire
Financial Strategies for All Ages to Navigate
Their Golden Years with Ease
by Robert Barbera

Ride Into the Sun
A Novel Based on the Life of Scipio Africanus
by Patric Verrone

Rita Levi-Montalcini
Pioneer & Ambassador of Science
by Francesca Valente

Saving the Republic
A Novel Based on the Life of Marcus Cicero
by Eric D. Martin

The Seven Senses of Italy
by Nicole Gregory

Sinner, Servant, Saint
A Novel Based on the Life of St. Francis of Assisi
by Margaret O'Reilly

Soldier, Diplomat, Archaeologist
A Novel Based on the Bold Life of Louis Palma di Cesnola
by Peg A. Lamphier, PhD

The Soul of a Child
A Novel Based on the Life of Maria Montessori
by Kate Fuglei

What a Woman Can Do
A Novel Based on the Life of Artemisia Gentileschi
by Peg A. Lamphier, PhD

The Witch of Agnesi
A Novel Based on the Life of Maria Agnesi
by Eric D. Martin

For more information on these titles and
the Mentoris Project, please visit
www.mentorisproject.org

Made in the USA
Middletown, DE
28 September 2022